AEGIS

The Shintori Chronicles: Book I

ELLE SAMHAIN

To my sister, the Mayhem to my Chaos.

TABLE OF CONTENTS

CONTENT WARNINGS

graphic violence

blood

gore

gun violence

monster horror

body horror

death and murder

PROLOGUE

All was still in the temple. Though the dark blanket of night was heavy, moonlight crept in through the stained glass windows and sent vibrant hues dancing across the marble floors. Grand depictions of the swirling sea and glittering night sky enveloped the hall in a sheet of indigo and turquoise.

She paced from left to right, a wisp of smoke in her shrouds of white canvas. The moon rose higher as she strode impatiently for an hour and the stories projected at her feet shifted. How long was she going to be kept waiting?

Suddenly the air around her creaked with the opening of a door and she froze. She felt the moonlight kiss her cheek warmly as if it gave thanks to the priestess for maintaining a calm demeanor. Straightening her back, she returned to the center of the transept and waited.

A black figure slunk through the tall wooden doors at the end of the prayer hall and into the moonlight. It stepped forward only a few feet before shifting with one knee on the ground in a sign of respect.

"Enter," she commanded.

With her permission, he stood up and began to approach her. He wore the hood of his black coat up, but she already knew who he was. Countless daggers and tools were strapped to both his waist and legs beneath the open coat. An elegant and slender sword sat in the back sheath that jutted over his shoulder. Though he was as armed as much as any other mercenary, she had nothing to fear. This man was devout to both the goddess Ara and Her priestesses.

He came no closer than five feet from her, his sharp jaw and stern mouth coming into view from under his hood. He knelt once more. "What is the urgency, Your Holiness?"

"The goddess of the earth has spoken to both myself and to the oracles of Neri," she began. "Yve declared that the last Knight of Od has finally arrived upon Her earth."

His mouth twisted with the angry growl in his voice. "Where?"

"That information was withheld from us. Perhaps to prevent Morgana and her Legion from finding the Knight before we do," she made every attempt to maintain her air of calmness as she spoke the wretched name. "She did, however, pass along something I think you'll personally find interesting."

"What is that?"

"Go to Ardua, the City of Illusion. There you are going to find a Reaper. Balthazar has said she will be of great benefit, both to our cause and to you personally. He did not elaborate as to why, unfortunately."

"Your Holiness, you're going to trust him? I wouldn't put it past that demon to set a trap."

"The goddess Mona trusts him, and I trust Her."

His jaw visibly clenched and he thought for a long moment before speaking. She could almost see the gears turning in his head as he formulated a plan. Upon his satisfaction he spoke.

"I'll put a hold on soul collections until this is done. I'm sure it will not have an adverse effect if the others do the same, Your Holiness."

She nodded. "Go at once. Return to me with the Reaper and we shall know where to find the last Knight. The other Knights will be waiting with eyes on you - you must move quickly."

CHAPTER ONE
THE FOOL

She looked down again at the ledger in her hands, and then back across the street.

Maybe she had lucked out and the man sleeping on the bench was already dead.

Then she saw the white orbs floating around his head and cursed to herself - *damnit, still alive*. His arms were folded neatly on his lap, his head tilted backwards, mouth agape. His flesh was beginning to turn pink; clearly he had found this basking spot a while ago.

It was likely that he would be there for some time. What a blessing it was, to be able to die in your sleep - while sunbathing comfortably, even.

"You're a lucky man, Hans Whitaker," she huffed as she crossed the street to approach him.

Killing him wouldn't attract the attention of the crowd moving in all directions of Usada street. She had tested it a countless number of times and found that all she really had to do was lay a hand on the person whose name appeared in her ledger. It could be a casual bump, a handshake, or an engaging conversation with a stranger. That was all it took to put their death in motion. Heart attack, traffic accident, suicide.

She'd seen it all in her short two months of being a Reaper - no death was less grim than the one before it. But if she had to pick a way to go, Mr. Whitaker had struck the death lottery.

She took a subtle scan of her surroundings, secretly hoping the man had a spouse or child around somewhere nearby. Then she couldn't kill him, she'd have to wait. It would just be too cruel for a man to be reaped in front of his kid. But there was no one. To all the people around, Mr. Whitaker was merely an article in the background. Her shoulders sank, her hopes of simply letting him live were dashed as she sat down next to him.

Grabbing the canvas bag she wore, she pretended to rummage through it clumsily and let a few of its contents dump onto the sidewalk.

She didn't think anyone would stop long enough to notice her, but she still put on the innocent display as she picked her notebook and apartment keys off the ground. Before sitting back up, the fingers of her left hand grazed Mr. Whitaker's ankle.

Moving quickly, she turned her head to see if she had disturbed the sleeping man. His head remained tilted upwards in the summer sun, chest rising and falling steadily. Still alive and still asleep, for now.

"Sorry, sir," she said and stood up. Not that a simple sorry would have made up for what she had really done.

Before she turned away, she opened the ledger once more to see the mysterious calligraphy that had spelled out his name. She caught it just before it had entirely vanished, leaving only a blank page. It was done.

A tightness gripped her in the chest, the effects of her guilt immediate. Would she become so jaded at some point that Reaping would be easy? Perhaps. She headed north on Usada Street, leaving Hans Whitaker behind.

Apartment buildings gave way to businesses as she entered the restaurant district of Ardua. She trudged along for two blocks before stopping at a sickeningly pastel cafe, glancing at the watch on her wrist and then up at the strangers passing her. Late again.

She spent longer than necessary re-tying the laces of her boot, both because of her fumbling fingers and her desire to stay out of sight for the time she was alone. When she could no longer justify the preoccupation, she straightened up, sighing and letting her shoulders drop.

Her hands still shook, the idea of murder still rattling her. She couldn't help but wonder what kind of man Hans Whitaker had been in life and what awaited him: punishment in Od or jubilance with the gods?

"Avery!"

She had been aimlessly kicking at air to pass the time and spun around at the call of her name. Her face lit up in a smile when she saw her friend pushing through the crowd, waving her hand in the air.

"Don't worry, Lily. I haven't been waiting long," Avery assured her friend.

Lily snorted. "Like I care with how heavy this backpack is. Wanna guess how many textbooks I took back today?"

"Too damn many?"

"Too damn many."

After they both had ordered their usual drinks they moved to one of the bistro tables outside and sat down in a pair of metal chairs, where she felt the warm relief of the sun on the skin of her legs. Lily began chattering about her research on metabolic disorders, but Avery was more entranced by the black orb hovering next to Lily's shoulders.

"Blood, blood, blood, blood, blood," the orb whispered in a small squeak, perhaps echoing Lily's mention of blood testing. Avery must have looked plenty distracted watching the sphere, and she snapped back to attention when Lily slowly stopped talking and frowned.

"I'm sorry, I'm probably boring you to tears."

"No!" Avery almost shouted, embarrassed that her distraction had been noticed. "I enjoy hearing about how hard you've been working." She chuckled a bit at herself as Lily smiled and carried on.

As they finished their drinks and left the cafe, giddy and laughing, Avery thought of the memories of laughter with her best friend that she received when she was put in this body. She only knew the memories of the person named Avery Porter as someone else watching from the outside of a foggy window.

"Can we go in here real quick?" Lily had stopped abruptly. Avery looked at the store sign to see it was a rather rundown convenience store.

She glanced at her friend. "Really?"

"Yeah, I just have to grab some pain relievers." She was already through the door before Avery could answer.

The fluorescent lights inside, reflecting off the crumbling white linoleum floor, gave the store a sickly green glow. She looked toward the sound of faint applause under the dull buzz of static and saw a game show playing on the television above the counter. A larger man in his middle years stood beneath the screen and met her gaze, pushing his glasses higher on his sweaty face. She turned on her heel slowly and paced down one of the tall aisles while Lily searched up and down a few more over.

Whether it was the buzzing of the drink coolers or the green cast of light, something was unsettling to Avery. She felt a stranger sensation of rocks at the pit of her belly and a wave of nausea overcame her. She rounded a corner to look in the next aisle.

"Lily?" Avery called out for her friend, hoping the panic in her wavering voice would go undetected.

"Calm down, it'll only take a second longer!" How like Lily to have noticed.

The sound of Lily's voice came from several aisles away and Avery hurried to meet her. Something in her gut shifted and she had a feeling that her friend needed to get out as soon as possible. As she passed another aisle quickly, she hit a hard surface, almost falling to the floor.

A metallic buzzing filled her ears, much higher pitched than the ambient sounds of the store. This wasn't a Reaping target she had just slammed into; those chimes were even higher pitched. The figure before her was tall, wearing a dark jacket and black jeans. It appeared to be a man, but for the black haze flying wildly around its face like a broken hive of frenzied wasps. All of the air left her lungs as she looked up at where the face should have been, trying to find any hint of humanity.

Was the man possessed by a demon of some sort? Whoever sent her here had told her of no such danger; this was neither a spirit haze nor a Marked soul.

Facial features finally began to seep through the dark haze as it faded. His eyes were hard and glared as if she had somehow insulted him; his jawline was equally sharp. The hard stare continued even when the haze was gone and Avery saw the white scar that marred the side of his left eyebrow. If she could guess his age, Avery would assume he was a couple of years older than her.

"Move."

His voice sliced the uncomfortable air that spanned the two feet between them. Avery looked at him incredulously, then at the clear fridge full of beer behind her. She gave him her most sour look and kept moving forward. Looking over her shoulder, she caught a glimpse of him disappearing behind an aisle with a twenty-four pack under his arm as Lily approached her.

"Who was that?"

Avery scowled and turned back towards her friend. "Some asshole. Let's get out of here."

The night did not settle on the city for several hours. Lily had retired to her room and had been hunched over her desk ever since they returned from the café, leaving Avery alone. Aegis, who had lived there since sometime before Avery was put in her body, replaced Lily's company.

The black cat was small for his age and something about the empty cranny in the bookshelf appealed to him. He sat there for the longest time while Avery nestled in a blue corduroy chair with a book; his eyes flickered between her and the front door whenever she looked up.

Music floated from down the hall, presumably from the couple two doors down. Avery finally sighed in defeat, putting down her novel and deciding she simply did not have the energy to go knock on their door. When she looked over, Aegis had moved his claimed territory from the shelf to the windowsill, blinking with glassy eyes down at the dark street below the second story.

"What do you see down there, little guy?"

She tried to pick Aegis up to cradle him but he lodged his claws firmly in the wood of the sill's surface in protest. Avery looked at him with bewilderment and let go. She looked outside and saw only a few people on the sidewalks and black orbs bobbing underneath the glow of the streetlamps. The lanterns from the apartments cast a red glow on the cracked pavement of the sidewalk before dissolving into darkness. She put her hands on her hips and frowned.

"Well if you're going to be so cold to me, I'm going for a walk," she sighed to the cat as if he would answer back. Avery made a mental note to kick this habit of hers; talking to her cat the way she did probably meant she needed to get out more.

She slipped her boots back on and turned off the living room lights. Aegis was sitting at her feet, sweeping his tail when she turned around. She smiled smugly with her arms akimbo as if she had won a silent face-off.

"That's what I thought, you bastard cat."

After putting her door key in her pocket, she placed Aegis into her jacket hood and walked outside. The air that greeted her was as warm and humid as it had been hours ago during her walk with Lily. Avery constantly reminded herself to take advantage of the warm weather with night exploration; she just never did. Reaping took a lot out of her by the time her tasks were done and whatever energy didn't go towards Reaping was spent during her shifts at the diner.

Night in the city of Ardua was like a whole other world when she stepped out onto the empty sidewalk. The warm glow of paper lanterns cast a comforting orange haze over ramen houses and secondhand stores. The soft hum of late customers and clanging pots flowed through arched, curtained entries.

The streets, earlier dense with people, had become promenades for the bobbing orbs. In some places they formed a black cloud while others basked under the streetlamps as though they were sunbathing.

"*Warm, warm, warm, warm, warm,*" one of them grumbled in a low hum.

She giggled until she caught notice of the man across the street, glancing in her direction before he continued to lock up a darkened store. Avery cleared her throat and began walking west. As Aegis leapt from her hood and walked alongside her, his head low to the ground, the thought occurred to her that perhaps he could see the orbs as well. After all, anyone who was superstitious claimed that animals are very sensitive to the supernatural. She walked with her arms swinging at her sides, the quiet and the warmth of the air lifting her spirits.

"See Aegis? Things aren't so bad! Maybe we can do this every night after I collect."

As the strange pair headed west, apartment buildings turned into boarding houses and began to stand a story or two taller as the alleyways between them grew wider. The dull hum of the restaurants became quieter until all was silent, aside from the occasional sound of a door being slammed indoors. Walking down the sidewalk, a faint orange glow fell from the inky sky and dissolved at her feet.

She looked up at a web of metal limbs above her and saw a woman perched in the fire-escape, the orange glow of a lit cigarette between her fingertips. The woman was maybe in her mid-thirties, a short bob of ginger hair framed her thin face. She wore a sundress made of a busy floral fabric that hung around her sinewy body like a bag. The woman stared back at Avery for a heavy moment before greeting her silently with a lift of two fingers.

A single black orb had been floating next to the woman's tucked knees, but nothing about that alarmed her. Yet the silent acknowledgement was unsettling; Avery pushed forward a little faster, her arms no longer swinging with gaiety.

From the other side of the street came a sharp whistle. "Aye, sweetie, what are you doin' tonight?"

She looked across the street to see a pair of men. Sweaty goblins in pitted-out work shirts catcalling her from across the avenue. Their grins were turned up in grotesque sneers as though that would invite her to sway right on over. Yeah, right. Avery clenched her right hand into a fist and raised her middle finger.

They hollered in amusement but Avery kept walking, knowing that they were more likely to give up and find someone else to bother than they were to follow her. She felt disgust curled in her lips still; sometimes she really hated the mortals.

As she walked, an orb that had been around her shoulders moved suddenly faster than her, gently pulling a long strand of her hair across it before falling over her shoulder. The shape disappeared around the corner of a building, yet Avery stood in shock at the revelation. Did these orbs have solid mass to them? She had never seen them come in contact with a person and she had assumed the orbs were no more of a hinderance than dust.

"Wait!"

She didn't think the orb was able to hear her or if it was even truly sentient. Avery rounded the corner and skidded down the alleyway where she saw an overflowing dumpster and a few broken pallets before it grew too dark to see. The orb bobbed around the dumpster before disappearing into the thick shadows. Avery's internal alarms sounded and her right foot stepped backwards, ready to take off in the opposite direction if needed.

A shadow moved forward, belonging to a human by the presence of legs that touched the ground. Her shoulders relaxed from their tense state and she felt a weight lift. She hadn't expected anyone to be this deep into a dark nook.

"I'm sorry! I thought I saw—" she began her excuse but stopped when she saw white eyes staring back at her. No irises, no pupils. Just white.

Aegis hissed at her side and the figure stepped all the way into her field of vision: a black humanoid shape, but as dark and translucent as the black orbs. It was easily a head taller than her, with long wiry limbs made of dark air. Her head buzzed with fear and she stumbled backwards. She knew for certain now that Aegis could see these entities and despite her expectation that he would run, he stayed within a few feet of her and hissed madly. The figure lunged at her with long arms and she shrieked.

Avery and Aegis began running, the cat always several paces ahead of her. She didn't want to turn to see if the shadow was still following, instead focusing on putting as much distance as possible between her and the alleyway. The streets were foreign to her in the dark and she didn't have a clue which direction Usada Street was as she frantically flew through intersections.

Her head ached with each pound of her feet on the pavement and she felt as though someone was holding her head down underwater as panic gripped her fiercely. As she ran, she glimpsed more white flashes of inhuman eyes emerging from fire escapes before they intensified their pursuit.

She would have run east if she'd known which direction that was. As they sprinted, she saw their movement like black flashes licking at her heels. Avery skidded and tore down a lighted alley on the side of a hotel, lanterns on the side of the brick and mortar wall. A shadowy figure lurched down from the alleyway, landing five feet in front of her.

Aegis at her feet was making noises that sounded like a cross between hissing and crying that she had never heard before. The lanterns had no effect on the inky darkness that the figures were made of. One reached out to her and she tried swatting the foggy arm away, her hand passing right through it with a sharp burning sensation. She looked down at her skin to find it bubbling pink and she yelped in pain.

Avery backed into the brick wall, looking up to calculate whether she could reach the bottom rung on the ladder of the fire escape. Or if it would even matter. The darkness closed in on her and she felt a wave of terror, expecting to be burned to a crisp. The terror came not from the heat and burning, but from the fact she knew that she would live through the whole thing. Harbingers of death don't die. Avery squeezed her eyes shut, waiting for the assault.

But it never came. There was a metallic ring and a ripping sound, followed by a shuffling of feet. Aegis stopped making whatever unholy sound had been coming from him and there were more ripping sounds. Avery opened one eye to see a tall, dark figure ripping a sword out of the middle of a shadow figure. This one was solid without a doubt, the light from above her head reflected off their black hood. Their back was to Avery and they swung the sword through two figures at once. The black shapes fell to the ground, seeping black liquid. Did these things have blood?

There were only two shadows left, lunging out for the person with their sinewy arms. They turned around and swung a foot at the ankles of one shadow, not seeming to feel the burning effect Avery did. Not only did they manage to knock it down, but they didn't pass through the shadow like she had; it was as though the shadows were suddenly made into flesh. They shoved the sword through the center of the shadow's head and the shining black liquid poured onto the pavement. As the last shadow pounced from behind, the sword-wielder whirled around so quickly that Avery hardly saw limbs moving as they severed the head from the body. It fell with a thud and the body followed.

The figure stood still with their back to Avery as she clutched Aegis against her chest. Her back was pressed against the wall and she couldn't stop trembling. They flicked their sword sideways in a swift movement, liquid darkness leaving the surface in splatters to reveal a clean, white blade. They stood in silence, not moving.

Avery moved to her feet and tried to slink away unnoticed. Aegis tried wriggling out of her arms but she clutched him tighter, freezing when the figure turned around. They sheathed the blade in the leather case strapped around their back.

"I wasn't —"she started before the figure lifted their hood and a shadow was cast over her from behind. Avery gasped in recognition.

"You!" was all she managed to say before a heavy thud to the head sent her spiraling into darkness.

— ❧ —

She felt heat in the back of her head but her eyelids were much too heavy for her to lift. Fatigue gnawed at her muscles and prevented her from moving across the itchy surface she felt beneath her left side.

Consciousness came back to Avery as slowly as a morning fog would leave a harbor and she became aware that she was still alive but could not confirm that revelation with her sight. There was a shuffling around her; footsteps that were much too heavy to belong to her roommate.

After five minutes or five hours of stillness— she couldn't tell which — Avery managed to open the eye that was not pressed against the fabric surface. In front of her appeared to be a short coffee table with only a lamp on top, its bulb bare and unobstructed by a shade. The light momentarily blinded her and she put up her hand to shield her until she could grow accustomed to the brightness. She caught a glimpse of movement from ten feet away.

"Looks like she's comin' to," a gruff voice of a man bellowed from somewhere around her.

She immediately dropped her hand and looked around at her surroundings to calculate any plausible escape routes. The walls were constructed lazily with red brick and sloppy mortar, uncovered by any attempts to make the space homier. The space was open and unobstructed by unnecessary walls, as she could see directly into what she assumed was a kitchen by the glow of a stove clock in the unlit room. It blinked twelve o'clock repeatedly as though whoever lived there had been too lazy to set it.

The only other light came from a lamp hanging above a small table littered with paper and books, with one chair pushed in neatly while the other was haphazardly placed a few feet away. She had been lain on a worn leather couch the color of milky chocolate and on the other side of the short coffee table was a chair of the same color.

Behind it stood a man- no, a human wall. The light of the lamp between them barely reached his face, the bottom half covered with a short ale-blonde beard that matched the hair that almost fell to his shoulders. His eyes were strangely jovial, though the glare from the light didn't allow her to assess the color. Avery took note of the dirt and black stains on his white shirt -- oil perhaps?

That was when she recalled the events that had transpired in the darkened alleyway. Avery looked around frantically for a door but there were none to be found through the dim light. Even Aegis wasn't able to be seen, if he was even there. This bastard could kidnap her if he pleased; after all, Avery knew he couldn't kill her. But if he dared harm Aegis, the fucker would meet a slow and painful end. Fury bubbled up inside her and she itched to vocalize it.

She let out a primal scream from somewhere deep within her and lunged for the lamp, grabbing its metal base and wielding it like a weapon. Avery swung at the man and saw his eyes widen before the swinging light cut her vision out and then in again.

"AYE!" He called out, dodging her blows but making no attempt to retaliate. She swung faster and put more might into her movement, desperate to make contact, but the flashing light made her target almost impossible to connect with.

"What… did … you … FUCKING DO," she screamed between swings and finally connecting a blow to what she thought was a shoulder.

The light bulb flew off and fell to the wood floorboards, breaking into shards. She was left in near darkness, the lamp hanging above the other table too far away to cast proper light on her target. She heard clumsy shuffling from the man's large feet, from her left and appearing to be backing away. Avery smiled, gripping the lamp tighter and stepped silently until she heard the crunch of glass.

An arm wrapped around her shoulders from behind and lifted her up off the floor. She felt cold metal pressed against her throat. The man in front of her appeared to be unarmed and he had much larger limbs.

"Don't move. You'll make it easier for both of us that way."

The voice that warned her was cold and flat. Fear welled up in Avery's throat and she felt trapped by the tall body against her. She wished she had a weapon of any sort -- not to necessarily defend herself with, because she didn't need that. No, she wanted a knife to make people like this pay. In her whole month in Ardua, why hadn't she thought of getting one?

"W-what are you going to do?" She said and laughed with loud nerves. "Kill me?"

She heard a snort coming from first man in front of her and then a laugh.

"She's almost as arrogant as you, Moz! Well I'd reckon that—aha, found it!"

An overhead light was flipped on and Avery shielded her eyes once again, dropping the lamp and wincing. She forced herself to look up. The first thing she saw in front of her was the first man, standing in front of a closed doorway next to a light switch. The light confirmed that he was, in fact, built like a giant. A hint of laughter lingered on his face as though he found the current predicament funny.

To his left was a hallway with three closed doors, their condition less than ideal, and a bookshelf lazily filled with books that appeared way too old to be safely opened. She saw Aegis poke his head out of a nook in the shelf, and her body eased a little with relief. "Would ya' let the girl down already? She's probably scared outta 'er mind!" the giant bellowed with a hearty laugh. The man holding her hesitated a short moment before setting her down.

"She's not scared; she's cocky."

When he released her, she immediately whirled around to see the young man sheathing the dagger.

His dark hair was messy, with long and wavy strands that shaded his forehead and nearly reached his eyes; the sides were cut shorter and cleaner. His jaw, clenched in anger, was hard and solid. In the corner of his left eyebrow was a whitened scar, contrasting with mossy irises.

She remembered him. It was the man from the convenience store whose black haze had frightened her. Now he had kidnapped her?

"What do you think you're doing?" she growled. "You'd be better off not messing with me."

"With you? You're not exactly threatening. You're five inches tall and I lifted you like a paper doll."

"You wouldn't dare hurt a —"

"A Reaper?" he interrupted and Avery froze, her eyes wide, thrown off guard. She didn't know if she should run or attempt to hit him over the head with a blunt object. He looked at her with an arched eyebrow, smug but still cold.

"That's what the aura was for. You saw that right?" He continued, seeming to know that she could not think of an equally sharp response. "Or did you think that you were the only one? Hate to break it to you, princess, there's a lot of us."

Her hand flew and connected with his cheek. His head turned with the blow and his cheek glowed red but he remained still just long enough for Avery to suck in sharp air of regret. When he turned and looked at her Avery started to backpedal, but he was much faster than she was. She barely realized he had moved until he had her arm twisted behind her shoulder and turned upwards. She felt him roll her leather sleeve as a sharp pain glided across the side of her wrist. Avery turned her head around and saw his dagger flick the surface of her burning skin, drawing vermillion beads to the surface. He tossed her arm away roughly, and she stumbled in the opposite direction towards the bigger man.

"Your first mistake was believing you're invincible," he jeered as he sheathed the knife once again. She looked down at the crimson blood leaking from her arm, not sure what to do or say. The three were quiet now and the dark-haired man shoved the itchy blanket off the couch Avery had been laying on and sat down. She felt a large hand on her shoulder and whirled around; the bigger man gently moved past her.

"Let me get ye' some water," he offered and moved towards the kitchen and flipped on the light. As he shuffled with glasses and pitchers, he kept talking.

"Like I said 'fore, that's Moz." Avery saw his head nod towards the dark-haired man. "Rhymes with 'grubby paws'. Not the friendly sort, but a well-seasoned Reaper."

The man talked about Moz as if he wasn't sitting there, and Avery saw a grimace spread over his face.

"And I'm Tristan."

He stepped forward and handed her a glass of water, Avery taking it in her shaking hands. She felt a warm brush against her leg and looked down at Aegis; he didn't seem alarmed in any sort of way. That didn't stop her from picking the cat up with one hand and placing him in her hood, she felt more comfortable with him near for some reason. The blonde giant gestured towards the leather chair.

"Have a seat, yer probably still exhausted. I made Moz keep the lights out so y' could rest, but that didn't last long."

She looked at him and hesitantly sat down in fear for what would happen if she didn't. Obviously these men were capable of harming her, the blood dripping down her wrist and into the crevices of her knuckles proved that much.

She looked over her shoulder at Tristan behind her. "Are you one, too?"

He let out another hearty laugh that emanated from his gut. Normally that much joy would make Avery feel good but it seemed Tristan only did this to make up for Moz's awfulness.

"Never!" He kept on laughing.

She felt heat rise in her cheeks again. These men were treating her as though she knew nothing. They were just lucky she was unarmed. Avery folded her arms and slumped into the seat, frustration showing on her face, as Aegis slinked into her lap to avoid being crushed against the chair.

"I'm an exorcist," Tristan continued, probably sensing her discontent. "I'm from the village to the west of here, Centralia."

Avery had never reached the city limits, let alone travelled to the towns she learned only fragments about in passing. She had a feeling her disbelief was showing on her face, as Tristan turned his brow up and Moz opened his mouth to speak before closing it with an incredulous expression.

"You mean, there are demons?" Avery tried to speak before either of them could, without realizing she probably just made herself appear more ignorant to her surroundings. Tristan looked at her thoughtfully before speaking.

"Aye, but not in the popular sense. Not according to superstition, anyway," he said. "They don't just emerge from the Beldam blades an' glory. But those black lookin' sprites you see everywhere? They aren't just floatin' around to look cute. They're looking for crippled souls to latch onto. Those shadow bastards y' saw? Used to be people long, long ago until they were completely taken over. It won't be long until they turn into complete beasts."

She blinked at him. "Beldam? What's a Beldam?"

Moz stood up violently, almost knocking over the table with his feet before he walked away, his fingers pinching the bridge of his nose in frustration.

"You know, this is great. We finally find another Reaper and her skull is full of rocks. Tris, we need to leave her behind."

He was pacing by the front door, looking ready to grab her by the hood and throw her out. She tried looking at the seemingly friendly one of the pair for an explanation, but was worried when Tristan's expression looked grim.

"Well," he began and Moz stalked off into the hallway. The large man sat down where the other had been sitting, his hands folded. "It appears t' me that you were kept ignorant fer some reason; my companion was let on to a lot more than you were."

"I lived in Centralia since I was a boy," he continued, "an' studied under the priestesses. They know about Reapers from the Origination Stories. You might want t' settle in for this."

Avery looked at him questioningly but sunk back in her seat with Aegis now cradled in her arms.

"There's a trio of sister goddesses. Our queen goddess, Ara, most people know an' still praise. She strived for purity in all things, healing the sick and punishin' the evil. I reckon if we imagine this as a sorta' hierarchy, below her was Yve. As the balanced one, she's thought to represent humanity and the turbulence o'nature. Mythology says her body was made into the physical earth, though we don't reckon that part holds any truth. The last sister was the very soul o'darkness: Beldam, the goddess of the underworld Od. She detested her sisters, knowing that Ara was favored by the gods and Yve was foolish."

"Humanity was something Ara wanted as the primary creator, but she would have made 'em perfect; Yve and the rest of the gods wouldn't have it, as they saw no purpose in perfect beings. Creating a sort of demi-god threatened her, as she and her husband Malo god of the forest, favored the balance they currently held. Beldam offered a solution of making the beings mortal-- their existence fleetin' as individuals, but lastin' as a group. She personally offered a group dedicated to upholdin' the mortal rotation. And thus death was created. Ara protested at first, and Yve pointed out that life may not be cherished if lived forever."

"They trusted Beldam as their sister. Ara refused to acknowledge the evil within her and Yve knew that fate would take its course no matter what. Reapers were born, placed throughout time in all places of the world. Beldam created the illusion of balance as Reapers collected the stronger, more spectacular souls, leaving weaker souls for demon consumption."

Tristan paused for a moment, giving Avery time to swallow the information. As his expression turned grim, she knew he wasn't finished. He cleared his throat and drank from his own glass before clasping his hands together.

"We've been in contact with Reapers around Brightloch who've noticed a startlin' trend of demons attacking humans, something we have never seen them do before. The High Priestess of Centralia theorized that the veil between the land of the living and the land of the dead, Od, is breakin'."

Moz came back into the room, and peered out the window around the black fabric curtains.

"I'd be able to relax if you didn't do all that screaming earlier, you brat. Who knows who heard," he mumbled to himself, turning slowly enough for Avery to see the dark expression he gave her. She sunk lower in her seat, but Tristan ignored his companion.

"What he means is, we would like y' to travel with us," he said, revising his friend's statement, smiling at Avery encouragingly.

"No. Absolutely not, that's another mouth to feed and slow us down. That's awfully inconvenient for someone who doesn't know anything and another body for me to protect from Leeches," Moz said with an icy tone.

Avery's cheeks flared; this punk was still talking about her as if she weren't sitting right there. When he walked past the back of the couch, she lurched up, dropping Aegis, and swung a fist at Moz with hopes of knocking some sense into him. That would show him he couldn't mess with her!

Moz grabbed her closed fist in his large hand before she even knew what was happening. He locked her in a death stare and his wiry fingers clenched, threatening to break every bone in her hand. The grip tightened and she wriggled to break free until the pain forced a whimper out of her. He let go of her hand, which was now throbbing and red, and turned away. For some reason, Tristan thought this was funny.

"At least she makes up fer lacked skill with gusto!"

Moz shot the same stare at his friend and the laughter stopped.

"Moz, you have to admit that it's strange she doesn't know as much as you and the others. The gods left her in the dark. There has to be a reason for it. I reckon we should take 'er with us?"

Moz looked as though he was thinking on the suggestion, his gaze shifting from Tristan to her. He frowned and finally spoke. "Getting her a weapon is going to be hard if we don't have coin."

Tristan's face lit up once more and he lifted his hand across the space between them as though it were nothing and ruffled Avery's hair, messing up her braid that threatened to come undone.

"She'll do y' proud I reckon!" Then turned his gaze to Avery. "Don't make me look like a fool, aye?"

She nodded, not knowing how else she was supposed to respond. Aegis meowed in the corner and she turned around. With eyes widened, she saw Aegis crouched on his front paws inspecting what appeared to be a large grey rat. Tristan's gaze followed hers and he called out.

"Aye, Moz!"

Moz turned around from where he'd been rifling through papers at the table and bounded the distance in two steps; Avery made a mental note to never try to outrun this long-legged punk. He reached down, scooped up the rat in his palm and set it on his shoulder. When he stood up he must have seen Avery's horrified look, for he scowled.

"What? You're not the only one who gets to keep a pet. Keep your feline away from Jack."

The rat looked at Avery with beady black eyes. His grey fur was spotted with white patches and his tiny nose twitched as he sniffed the air. The expression on Moz's face didn't change as he stalked back into the hallway and through the door that he had entered earlier.

Tristan huffed, sending a strand of his blonde hair upwards. Sitting back down again in the chair, he confessed, "I wish I could say that his attitude gets better with time, but I don't really know." He reached down to pet Aegis, who was slinking up against his thick ankles.

"It's late in the night and tomorrow you need to say your goodbyes. So I reckon you get some real rest," he advised and stood up to leave.

"Neither of you let me decide if I was going with you. In fact, you haven't even told me why," Avery murmured with realization of the fact the two men had bickered and babbled with only a word or two from her. "I'm not going to get up and leave with two strangers."

She grabbed Aegis up off the floor, ready to flee the moment Moz wasn't looking. Tristan blocked her like a brick wall, placing one hand lightly on her shoulder.

"I'm really afraid I can't let y' do that. I can't offer you an explanation now, but I need you to trust that we can't leave you in the city. I will owe you one once it's far behind us."

Avery backpedaled away, her heart pounding violently in her earlobes. "You-you're abducting me?"

The way Tristan laughed at her words made her face flush with anger and she reached out to swipe him across the face. He dodged her, his movements not as fluid as Moz's but enough for her to be swatting at air.

"Look, me and the boy have done far worse. I won't lie to ya, kid. But after tonight, I reckon it wouldn't be in yer best interest to stay in Ardua. Consider this a favor."

Her temple throbbed and she held the corners of her mouth tightly in a firm frown, stretching across the rest of her face. Moz was only supposed to collect souls as a Reaper, and Tristan should only exorcise under the Priestesses. Moz's barely-hidden agenda made her stomach churn. At least Tristan had looked at her with sincerity as he explained.

Avery's heart sank, realizing she had already been overpowered twice trying to escape and that a third attempt would be futile. The two men appeared to know a lot more about Ardua's landscape and alleyways than she; even if she did manage to escape, they would find her, lost, and drag her back to their filthy apartment. Avery's mind flashed with the images of Moz's sword cutting through the demons as if they were made of paper. Her ears began to ring and for a brief instant her core ached with the idea of that same sword slicing through her. Tristan may have a little sympathy for her, but Moz had none.

If she played nicely, she could wait until Tristan gave her the information she wanted and she could escape to a neighboring city.

Tristan saw her inner gears turning and ducked his head down to reach her eye level. "What's yer name, kid?"

"Avery," she muttered, almost as though she didn't want Moz to overhear. The giant smiled and stood up straight again, towering over her.

"Well Avery, why don't y' get some rest. I know you'll take the right path." He walked to the switch he'd stood at moments ago, flipped it off, and shuffled down the dark hallway, leaving her in darkness.

The butt of a cigarette was smashed angrily into the metal dish sitting on the desk, the grand cherry wood furnishing the only piece in the dimly lit room. She folded her wiry arms across her chest, suited and dressed to the nines. Her left leg twisted around in front of her right, confined by the width of the grey pencil skirt. As she grimaced in disgust, the uniformed man in front of her seemed to use every ounce of self-control to not shake. She shook her head again, but not a strand of her ginger bob fell out of place.

"You're only assuming she's exhibiting free will now?" She growled angrily. "Mosley found her, and I thought I explicitly said to isolate him from any other

Reapers. That punk is poison, and the last thing I want him to do is come in contact with anyone else. Why couldn't he have been taken care of when I ordered it in the first place?"

The young man was rather small compared to her other subordinates, but she knew he was fast on his feet. That was more than enough to make up for a little vertical disadvantage. His lower lip trembled before he spoke, carefully choosing his words.

"Commander, we have not let up on Mosley since he was first identified as a threat. It's like he's always a step ahead and we—"

"Then move faster," she snapped and lit the newly rolled tobacco, the initial puff of smoke concealing her face for a moment.

The man cleared his throat nervously and continued. "I still believe we can get him to succumb without needing to kill him, but the Reaper he came in contact with may complicate things."

The commander blew out a long stream of smoke aimed above her head. Perhaps catching that snake would have been simpler with a reliable crew.

"Have it your way. We'll make room for Mosley. But never give him the chance to find the missing piece."

Her subordinate bowed in respect before she added, "Prevent them from leaving Ardua within reasonable cost. If they cause too much of a fuss, we'll slip away quietly. They can only run so far."

CHAPTER TWO
THE MAGICIAN

Deep sleep wasn't hard for Avery to find that night, but the slight stirring of Aegis on her stomach woke her up. She rubbed her eyes and pushed away hair from her face that had fallen free of her braid, the cat watching her with glassy eyes. There was a shuffling movement around where she laid on the couch and Avery propped herself upward to look.

Both men were awake and already stuffing a pair of leather packs with knives, wrapped food, and several other objects she couldn't identify. She stood up, the loose waves of her hair falling around the middle of her ribcage as Aegis leaped onto the floor and approached Tristan's heels cautiously. Moz was stuffing a pile of clothes in his leather pack and Tristan was buckling his own shut when he looked up at her.

"Aye, we've been waiting for y' Avery!" he gushed and hung the pack on his shoulder by its single strap. Moz grimaced, maybe at the realization that she had a name, and she felt her eyebrows furrow. He closed his pack as well after placing Jack inside on a flattened ball of clothing. The pack was slung over the top of the sheathed sword he strapped to his back.

"Grab the cat," he commanded. "We're departing immediately."

Avery picked up Aegis, not out of obedience but in alarm. "His name is Aegis… and I'm not leaving with you."

Moz huffed in annoyance and shook out his hair with his hands. "Look kid, originally we were going to give you options. But you're wearing my patience thin, and it's already pretty fuckin' minimal. You're going outside and you will see what kind of danger you're in just for coming in contact with us."

Her eyes widened, remembering her conversation with Tristan the night before and she looked with wide eyes at the biggest of the pair. He regarded her with a soft gaze and nodded, confirming what Moz said.

"You're kidnapping me because of something you did before?"

As she pleaded, Moz grabbed her arm and tossed her into the hallway.

"WHAT DID YOU DO?" Her question came out as a scream. When she hit the beige wallpaper Moz's hand clamped over her mouth tightly.

"Avery," he said in a low voice. She didn't like the way her name sounded coming from him, as though he had turned it around in his wiry hands a few times before deciding whether or not it was a name.

"You're going with us, whether by your own accord or forcibly. You're going to tell us where you live, and we'll go get you warmer clothes. By this time, you will see the people trying to kill us, you too now. You can say goodbye to whoever you need to if there is time. When I drop my hands, you will not scream."

It wasn't a question, but Avery still nodded. Moz dropped his hand and she seized the opportunity to threaten him.

"If you do that again, you're losing a finger."

He ignored her threat, and Tristan ushered her down the hall to follow Moz. The hallway seemed intact compared to the inside of the men's apartment, although a sickly glow similar to that at the convenience store emanated from the fluorescent lights. Remembering Moz's initial expression there made her stomach turn. She scowled and shook her head, trying to center her attention on the hall before her.

They shuffled in a line down the stairs, Tristan's large frame behind her making it rather uncomfortable for people passing in the opposite direction within the narrow hall. Each time they heard footsteps from a flight below, she noticed Moz's right hand lift slightly, constantly alert. Finally they reached the ground floor and he pulled a set of keys from his jeans pocket. Avery's eyebrow raised, skeptical that he rightly owned it once she saw the make name on the big key fob.

"So the big problem is that you steal c—"

She was cut off when he turned around with an acidic glare, one hand on the handle of the glass door.

"I'm going to get the car and pull it up here. More than one of us will attract too much attention; they'll be trying to spot Tristan first," he called before disappearing into the blinding sunlight.

Tristan grabbed her elbow gently and pulled her away from the door, before she yanked herself out of his grip.

"Don't ye worry none," he assured her, despite her lack of concern. "He'll be back quickly."

Moz strode into the next alley with a casual demeanor, knowing that the Leeches would be looking for feelings of alarm or panic. His eyes searched rapidly without a single turn of his head, but there were no shadows to be seen in the sun-drenched façade of the apartment complex.

The small, squat car sat on the side of the alley nearest the vacant building next to the apartments. He approached the car, circling it with a hand on the hilt of his blade until he was confident that he was alone. The blue towel and spilled office files remained in the backseat, untouched despite the car having been lifted from a parking lot.

It was modest for a car despite the fact that only Ardua's wealthiest inhabitants were lucky enough to have one. The car had been sitting in this alley for nearly three days, and he was fully aware that the police department of Ardua knew it was there. But they knew better than to take an eager approach.

He ducked inside the car, and although he wasn't as tall as Tristan he still sat in an uncomfortable shrug. Moz looked at the steering wheel, sharply inhaling before turning his attention to the gearshift. He had only driven a car once before lifting this one and had to recollect instructions given to him by another Reaper.

"Damn, Kurosaki," he growled to himself. "A diagram might have been helpful."

He sat for a full two minutes with the keys in the ignition and the engine running before he remembered. Once the car rolled forward, he felt comfortable again. Picking up speed, he spun the car around the corner and came to a screeching halt in front of the glass door of the apartment building. Tristan's face had been peeking out from the side and after he saw the car he vanished momentarily before ushering the girl outside before him.

She had been wide-eyed the entire time, he assumed out of both ignorance and fear. It wasn't too late to just leave her behind; Morgana wasn't going to hold back any longer in her pursuit of his faction and one slip-up from this kid could be the end of it all. The thought made him grimace and he was half-tempted to lock the doors before she could climb into the backseat, but before he could, she was already scrambling inside.

"Alright Avery, where do y'live?" Tristan asked, hunching forward to fit in the front passenger seat. Her eyes widened in such a timid way that it seemed for a moment that she'd completely forgotten where she lived before finally reciting her address. Moz had expected the address to belong to a more upscale district of Ardua by the way she dressed and had reacted to their apartment, but it was in the part of town only slightly better than his. The car jolted forward, sending their bodies lurching forward then back before the movement smoothed down. Tristan grimaced at him.

"Yer gonna kill us before they do!"

Avery pulled the key ring out of her pocket when they reached her apartment door, Tristan and Moz hovering behind her in a wall formation. She felt Aegis shuffle around again in the hood of her jacket and she knew the two men made him uneasy.

She knew a rather easy way to make her escape; she'd enter her room, pretending to gather her things so she could lock her door behind her and call the police using the telephone on her desk.

She unlocked the door and entered first. The apartment appeared just as she had left it; the warm glow of the lamps in the center living room and the sight of her book still on the coffee table comforted her. Lily's endless stack of folders had also been moved to the table.

The instant relief she had felt suddenly washed away and Avery's heart pounded; she prayed that the two men would not take any interest in Lily. Would they hurt her for being here? Or was she beyond their scope?

"H-hello?" She called out and stepped forward. "Lily?"

Aegis jumped out of her hood, clearing the three feet between Avery and the kitchen bar. Avery heard the shuffling of feet at the end of the hall to the left, where both hers and Lily's rooms were. Her roommate's door opened, and Lily emerged in grey sweatpants and a t-shirt.

"Avery! Where have you been?"

Lily moved into the center of the apartment where they had been standing, and her eyes widened as she took notice of the two men standing behind Avery. Lily's expression changed from exuberant to cautious with a raise of her eyebrow. Avery noticed only after Lily's gaze shifted to where Moz stood.

"Avery, who are your friends?"

She took a single step back when Avery's eyes widened. Avery did all she could to express her own alarm without doing so verbally, since neither of the men could see her face as she stood in front of them.

"We're Avery's coworkers," Moz answered for her coldly. She tried to picture Tristan's burly figure waitressing tables on roller skates and for once was thankful for her shitty day job; it was a dead giveaway that something was wrong.

Avery saw Lily's deep umber face harden with skepticism, and her own expression grew as alarming as she could possibly make it. Lily finally looked in her eyes, and Avery mouthed as slowly and clearly as she could: police.

Lily waited a moment before nodding once slowly and Avery knew her message had been understood. But she carried on as though the nod was a response to Moz's statement.

"I haven't met any of her coworkers yet, she likes to keep her work life separate from leisure!" Her expression looked relaxed, but Avery knew better. She started shuffling towards the kitchen. "I wasn't expecting Avery to come back with guests, and this early too! Let me get you both something to drink."

Aegis was perched in front of the coffee maker, blocking Lily from it before she shooed the cat away. "Stubborn feline! Avery, please come feed your little prince, I know he was with you and I doubt you fed him."

Avery moved into the kitchen and neither Moz nor Tristan prevented her; although Tristan explained, "We brought her over here to get some clothes, the staff is going on a retreat. Why don't y'go do that?"

Waiters? On a retreat? She could have laughed - what did they think she did for money?. Avery saw the alarm in Lily's face now before it was hidden again, and there must have been something in the way Tristan spoke that made her even more afraid. She didn't like the way he pushed her away from Lily's request to get Avery into a different room.

There was no way Avery was leaving her friend alone with these two, yet her resistance might become known if she refused. Her panic was broken by her friend laughing. Lily had been looking down at the counter while she toyed with something, presumably with the coffee grounds but the bulky machine was in the way. She looked up from the counter with a feigned grin that only Avery recognized.

"That's okay! I'll feed him! Avery, before you go pack, please…"

Moz was walking toward her now, and she trailed off mid-sentence. Lily's eyes widened with fear and she backed up into the counter as he approached her, shaking when she realized she had nowhere left to escape to. He pushed her aside, not violently but forcefully enough to move her a few feet from where she had been standing.

The kitchen telephone was off the hook, and the small buzzing of the person on the other line could be heard over the dead silence that fell upon the room. He picked up the phone, small in his large and wiry hands. With a simple click, he hung up the phone and looked at Lily.

"You called the cops, didn't you?"

Without hesitating, Avery lunged for the knife block on the opposite counter, and Moz swiftly changed his position so he was facing both girls as Avery held the biggest knife available in front of her. She pointed it at him, slowly stepping sideways until she was between him and her friend. His expression was hard and alert, much as it had been in the convenience store.

He said nothing, holding a short blade now out of the side of his right fist and Avery couldn't recall him ever pulling it out. It was not aimed at them; Moz did not find them threatening but felt the need to have it drawn as Avery's hand quivered, clutching her own knife in front of her. It was silent for a long moment as he watched her with cold eyes before he spoke.

"You're even dumber than I thought," he said, his voice's flatness more threatening than the words he spoke.

Moz made no advance towards the pair, but Avery felt Lily quivering behind her and realized they were backed as far into the counter as they could be. She wished that somehow the cherry wood would bend behind their weight and allow them to slink out of Moz's reach.

"Tristan was wrong, you don't have any guts. Nor skill."

Avery had completely forgotten Tristan, despite his large size he became lost in the background of the dissension. She sensed his bulky form in her periphery, yet her attention remained focused on trying to anticipate Moz's next move. In the confrontation she barely noticed the loud thuds coming from outside. Moz's slightly crouched form straightened.

"Tris," he ordered.

Tristan nodded and moved to the windows before pushing aside one of the gauze curtains. Avery's focus didn't move with him, but she could still sense the giant's alarm.

"Unfortunately fer us, they've improved their response time," he grumbled before stepping away from the window and drawing his own blade, a darker steel than Moz's and curved towards the top.

Moz's expression didn't change, but Avery could feel he was reluctant to end the impasse. He didn't sheath his blade, but instead lowered his arm completely. Avery wasn't sure if she should be relieved or angered that she wasn't seen as a threat.

"If you want to protect your friend, we need to leave now," he announced. "They want us, not her. You have about ten more seconds to grab your things for a time gap large enough."

Avery rarely acted without hesitation but somehow she was able to pull herself forward with realization. If they could leave quickly enough, whoever threatened them would not even come across Lily and she would not be endangered.

Avery stumbled through the door of her room, almost falling on the way inside. Her fingers ripped open her brown canvas and leather rucksack, dumping out its contents without looking at them on the wooden floor. She fumbled around in her closet and stuffed in a pair of black jeans before lurching across the room to grab her black book and pencils, shoving them inside as well.

Her eye caught the photograph on the desk just long enough to feel the heartache. Avery and Lily's young faces, grinning in green graduation gowns and surrounded by Lily's family. *No, my family.* She gave herself a mental wrist-slap and snatched up her plastic water bottle on the desk before fleeing the room.

Moz and Tristan were already in the doorway waiting for her, on their toes and ready to push their way out of the building. Avery scooped up Aegis in her arms; he seemed to be waiting for her in the right place to do so while still moving forward. She gave her friend one last look, Lily's face painted with astonishment and fear from where she still stood in the kitchen.

"I'll come back, Lily. I promise," Avery said softly before disappearing with the two men into the hall.

Tristan was waiting for her on the left of the door, with Moz on her right now. He turned his dagger around, jammed it into its leather sheath and held it out to her.

"In the unlikely event you get your shit together, defend yourself," he growled. She took it into her hand just as he unsheathed his sword and moved forward. Tristan pushed her to follow him from behind before the trio took off in a sprint.

"You threaten my sister and then hand me a knife? You have a fucking death wish."

"Your sister?"

Avery heard the skepticism in his voice and scowled. People were always quick to comment on the different complexions in one way or another.

"I'm adopted, you idiot."

Avery was drunk with adrenaline and on a few occasions almost tipped over, feeling as though the ground beneath her had crumbled. It remained firm under her feet and she pushed forward. With Aegis in one arm and the dagger held out in front of her, she focused on Moz's back as they ran to the end of the hallway. He stopped suddenly as uniformed figures flooded the bottom of the only staircase.

"Keep going down the stairwell," he barked, bounding over the half-wall and jumping to the ground. She did not see what happened after, but she kept moving forward until she reached the stairs. Tristan followed as they stumbled hurriedly down the steps until they reached the bottom.

Moz ripped his blade out of an officer's chest and Avery heard the screams of people in the nearby area. At his feet were three bloodied bodies, four when this particular one fell. He stepped around them in a deadly dance, the remaining two officers circling him with their swords to get a better angle at Moz's throat.

A blonde woman appeared to be keeping up with his pace, and her movement finally positioned her behind Moz while he stared down the burly man in front of him. She lunged at his back, sword ready to plunge through his heart. Avery froze, conflicted about whether or not she should yell out a warning.

Without turning to face her, Moz shoved his sword with sharp force past his side to strike behind him. The blade plunged through the woman's throat and out the base of her skull. Avery gasped and squeezed her eyes shut as though it would block out the horrific gurgles and final thud.

In the flurry of chaos, Tristan ran forward and sunk his own blade into the other man. The officer remained standing, but Tristan already knew it would take more than one stab to drop this giant. He took advantage of the brief moment of surprise washing over his opponent's face and shoved the officer into the support beam of the second story, his hand remaining on the hilt and pulling it out. With one more stab to the chest, the man finally sunk to his knees before falling face-first onto the pavement wet with crimson.

Avery searched for Moz, who was already weaving through police vehicles toward their stolen car. He flicked his sword, blood splattering off it like it had during their previous meeting. Tristan ran ahead and jumped into the passenger side; Avery had barely gotten into the car before Moz was reversing.

She had yet to put on her seatbelt and was thrown to the opposite side of the cabin when the car lurched to the left. She careened forward and placed her right hand on the floor to push herself back upright, clutching Aegis tighter with her left. As she hastily locked herself in with the seatbelt, she watched Moz momentarily fumble with the gearshift.

"Don't you know how to drive?" she shouted over the cacophony of the tires screeching against pavement as they accelerated.

"Nope," Moz uttered simply.

Her eyes widened, her stomach somersaulting as they shifted around the corner. Avery leaned against the window on her right to look ahead and saw people on the sidewalk in a rushed panic, pushing their backs against shop windows to get as far away from the scene as possible. Even the bobbing black orbs seemed to react, but they were moving toward their car rather than avoiding it. When she looked forward she noticed that the car was careening incredibly fast through the city grid.

"Moz, that was a stop sign," she jeered as he flew through yet another intersection without any sign of slowing down, her knuckles on her right hand whitening as she gripped Tristan's seat in front of her and the other hugged Aegis a little tighter.

"Do you ever shut up," Moz growled at her, the agitation thickly lining his voice.

She felt her face furrow with frustration, and the car harshly swerved another ninety degrees as they turned a corner. The rucksacks on the floor shifted, and she held her dagger firmly under her foot to keep it from pitching across the unsteady cabin. She saw Jack, the gray rat that had been in Moz's rucksack, wriggling out of the loose opening.

Knowing the animal could be seriously injured or killed if Moz turned too sharply again, she leaned as far as she could while still restrained by the seat belt and picked Jack up with her right hand. Under her fingers she felt his tiny racing heartbeat, but his spotted fur was much softer than she had anticipated. Initially, the rat squirmed in alarm so she set him down in her lap with her hand, petting him but never lifting her hand too far in case she had to suddenly grab him. Aegis stared at the creature curiously, his throaty purr vibrating against Avery's hand. She wanted to tell Moz that she had probably saved his pet but decided she shouldn't push his temper any further.

The wail of sirens erupted behind them, growing nearer every second. Avery turned to look over her shoulder and saw that the cacophonous fleet was closing in on them quickly. How long would it take until they rammed into their getaway sedan or cut off their escape path? Surely they would use their reinforced bumpers to create damage before they entered into sword combat, maybe even with intent to kill using the vehicles. Moz and Tristan had just slaughtered several officers in broad daylight; she doubted the police would ask for explanations.

The surroundings became less familiar to her as they approached the outskirts of Ardua and drove toward places that Avery had never bothered to venture into. She held onto Aegis a little tighter, her hand cupping over Jack in her lap as the car swerved and caused a van travelling in the opposite direction to screech to a halt. Moz only continued to accelerate.

The car turned onto a road that ended with a grey, brick wall. It must have stood at least six stories tall and towered over the buildings it held within and Avery wondered how she could have possibly missed this marvel. As they hurtled ever-faster toward the wall, she could see a grand metal gate, closed to whatever lay beyond. Moz's intentions became clear and she realized they were not going to simply exit Ardua and reason with the armed guards that flanked the gate.

"You're going to kill us all!"

She pulled the two animals toward her with one arm and used the other to brace herself against the door, awaiting the impact of the hood of the car with the metal gate long before it would even happen. The rear view mirror reflected Moz's lips curled into a sinister smile. It was the first smile she'd seen on him and she prayed it would be the last. Her stomach turned as he showed his teeth before pursing his lips shut again. She put both the animals inside her own rucksack to cushion them as best as she could, Aegis cried out in protest as she hugged the back against her chest.

The impact of the bumper hitting the metal gate sent Avery crashing into the side door, her head bouncing off the plastic frame. Screeching metal warped all around them, the world collapsing at a violent speed. The windshield shattered and glass exploded in the cabin, hitting Avery's face. Blood bloomed from her cheek. Their bodies rattled from the jolt as they passed through the now gaping gate, Tristan regaining his stability first with his large frame.

"Av'ry, get ready to run. Stay armed. We go as far as the road takes us and then we get out," he instructed, putting his rucksack over his free shoulder while keeping one hand gripped on the dashboard. She looked over behind them at the police cars, now stopped firmly in the open gate.

"They've stopped?"

The city and its walls gave way to tall, dry grasses. Avery saw the red symbols painted on the bricks of the outside wall. Their geometry made Avery uneasy - they had an esoteric intention about them. She turned forward and saw that about a mile ahead of their car, the bubbling green of a forest sat awaiting for them like an animal with an open mouth. Their path was paved, but only halfway. Pavement gave way to gravel before becoming grass about a mile from their destroyed bumper.

"It's because they know better than to follow," Moz said.

For the first time, his voice wasn't dripping with malice or discontent. His serious tone was subtle, but it was enough to raise alarm.

Why would they not follow? Were they driving toward certain death? She looked out the gap where the window used to be, the wind of speed howling through the empty silence Moz left. The flattened trail disappeared from under the tires and the grinding of gravel added to the noise before they jolted to a halt, the metal bumper banging as it hit a large stone.

"Now's as good a time as any, aye?" Tristan chimed with agitating optimism and threw open his door.

Avery got out of the car, grabbing her dagger off the floor and swinging her rucksack onto her back, flinching when she remembered Jack and Aegis were still inside. Moz put his own pack on his back and looked behind them at the walled city, now less menacing than it was from the inside.

"They've got a death wish," he said of the trio of cars that were pulling out from the gate towards them while leaving the others behind.

Tristan had already taken off into a sprint towards the open mouth of the forest. Knowing her endurance wasn't as up to par, Avery began after him.

Her feet slid as gravel gave way from the slight decline and she skid forward. Tristan was charging forward, bull-like, as he carried his large sword. Her footing broke and she slid downward, landing on her palms. She winced and hissed as small pebbles embedded painfully into the skin of her hands.

"Keep running!" She heard from behind her.

Avery looked over her shoulder at Moz, his blade drawn and running past her with such long strides that he barely made contact with the earth. For a moment she was unsure he had spoken. The words were deep and full-bodied, unlike Moz's usual cold remarks. Without wasting any more time she scrambled to her feet to sprint, moving with ease across the patch of levelled ground.

Avery's lungs burned with fatigue as they ran, crashing through the branches as Tristan led the trio with his large sword held defensively in front of him. Her knees buckled once again, slowing her down momentarily and Moz shouted in frustration from behind her. She kept up with Tristan despite every muscle fiber begging for her to sit down and breathe. They had sprinted for at least fifteen minutes since breaking the edge of the trees and there were still no signs of any police officers trailing them.

She yelled out, "Can we… PLEASE… stop so someone… can EXPLAIN" with staggered breaths.

"Wait only a little longer, we're almost to the riverfront."

She didn't answer whoever had just spoken but pushed on with aching muscles and tendons. The forest around them buzzed with life, birds talkative in the canopies of the elms. They pummeled the brush as they ran and the occasional animal fled with the crack of branches and crunch of leaves under their small paws. Only a brief moment after she heard the rich voice, the sound of a river became faint. Faster and faster she ran, and the whispering water became a roar.

The terrain declined once more until the trees gave way to a rocky shoreline of the river, its might sending rolls of thunder as it crashed against large rocks. Moz and Tristan were already on the beach, looking around with their weapons drawn as she scuttled down the rocks to them.

"The river's too deep to ford here," Tristan croaked between huffs of exhalation, while Moz seemed strangely comfortable. "We need t' find some way of crossing."

The shouts of their pursuers crashed through the trees, much louder than they were when the trio had been sprinting downhill. Panic welled in Avery's throat and she looked about frantically.

"The river runs southward, follow it."

She sensed a presence from behind her with a tingling sensation on her temples, but turned around to only see Moz facing uphill with his back to her. Whoever it was had been right about the riverfront and she couldn't ignore this second piece of advice. Tristan was already wading into the water, but paced backwards when he decided he was no match for the depth or might of the water.

"Follow it south," Avery relayed and began scrambling across the rocky beach in the direction the water was flowing.

She saw Tristan's skeptical glance towards Moz as she passed them but she didn't bother to turn for any confirmation. Tristan splashed loudly in the water as he trudged over the waterline to follow her.

"Keep going, I'll follow," she heard Moz's voice call out from behind them.

She looked over her shoulder to see him finally pushing forward from where he had been standing still for the longest time, just looking at the trees. The shouts became clearer, belonging to different males and perhaps one female. Moz swore loudly, somehow much closer to Avery and Tristan now.

In some places the beach gave way to small cliff sides that they climbed easily, using the protruding tree roots as footholds. In other areas, the beach disappeared completely. Avery's feet ached in her soaked boots as they trudged through the shallow water. The entire time neither of the men voiced any doubt over Avery's choice of direction. She thought for sure Moz would at least be quick to argue against any input from her.

"Avery was right!" Tristan shouted and pointed ahead.

Fifty yards ahead of them, the river narrowed beneath the short cliffs. Connecting them was a fallen elm, long dead and bare. Its entire root system sat perched on their side of the river. He ran ahead of her, eager to cross the river.

"Tristan crosses first to test stability," Moz stated. "Can both of you swim?"

She didn't bother to answer, her lungs heaving as she ran faster. The shouts behind them became clearer; glancing past Moz, Avery could see their figures running along the beach. How were they catching up so quickly?

By the time she scrambled up the small cliff to reach the natural bridge Tristan was already climbing the fallen trunk, moving slowly to keep his footing, his sword held as a balance across him. Avery gripped the roots as if she could somehow keep the entire elm steady and her hands were immediately coated in soil.

"When he's halfway, start crossing," Moz instructed as he climbed over the top of the cliff, his long legs driving him upward with ease. His voice remained flat but focused as he turned his back to her, facing their pursuers. Avery looked ahead and saw that Tristan had crossed more than half of the tree.

She climbed onto the trunk, her dagger in hand as she pushed herself up with the pads of her fingers. Willing herself not to look down, she stepped forward with her right foot and dragged her left across to meet it, keeping one foot planted at all times.

"Okay," she said aloud to coach herself through. "You're going to have to go faster than that."

Despite her own advice she repeated the same step-and-drag action. After a couple repetitions, she was able to carry herself to the halfway point, her body crouched low to avoid being blown over by a gust of wind that swept through the ravine.

"MOSLEY!" A deep voice belonging to one of the attackers bellowed from behind her.

This was enough to frighten her to push forward, and she straightened up and immediately ran across the remaining length of the trunk. Tristan reached out to grab her by the wrist, yanking her hard onto the bank. She turned around once she felt the relief of solid ground under her feet.

Moz remained on the trunk, perched with ease despite the wind catching the longer tendrils of hair on the top of his head. He was stepping backwards to cross the last third of the trunk's distance, his sword pointed toward the people on the opposite bank.

At the front of their group was a young man who appeared unthreatening, apart from the dark steel sword he held. She couldn't make out finer details from across the distance, but Avery did take note of his shaved red hair and thick-rimmed glasses. He was flanked on on his left by a taller man with tan skin and blonde hair shorn in the same fashion. On his right was a young woman with dark, shoulder-length hair. "This isn't like you, William." The officer spoke again, not as booming as it had been before but loud enough for Avery to hear over the roar of the river. Moz kept stepping backwards with ease, clearly a seasoned swordsman.

"You bring calamity wherever you walk, yet is this you fleeing I see?" The man continued, never daring to climb over the roots to pursue Moz on the tree. "If you go any farther, I will be forced to slaughter your companions. All of them."

"You getting promoted anytime soon, Pete? You've always come so close to getting us, never quite made it, though. My companions are well hidden." Avery could hear Moz's smirk as he laughed.

He held his sword with a more aggressive stance now, crouching lower as the officer stepped onto the trunk. Tristan grabbed Avery by the shoulder and pulled her backwards, away from the ledge.

"They won't cross the river," he noted. "But yer going to want to keep a safe distance."

The other officer charged at Moz, the heavy metal of his sword clanged against Moz's blade. As they danced it became clear that, although his opponent was bulkier, Moz was quicker. The man lunged towards Moz's torso with his weapon, meeting Moz with a metallic shriek. Moz twisted like a snake until he was able to slide away and plunge his sword through the officer.

A push deeper completely impaled the man, and Avery gasped as she averted her gaze. Avery knew that the next thud was of the body hitting the tree and she peeked after the splash that followed. The sword in Moz's hand flicked sideways, splatters of blood flicking away from the blade. He now stood with his sword pointed at the remaining officers, not as a raise of defense but as a warning.

"You sent her goons after me, but you didn't think to send archers?" Moz's shouts were monotone but held an eerie weight that made even the trees hush. "Send me everything you have next time; I'll kill them all. Let Morgana know."

Moz stood out on the trunk of the tree long after the two officers had retreated, still holding his sword at his side as he listened. Avery remained frozen, afraid to move until Moz relaxed. Tristan remained with her in the brush, his sword held out as well. Her sweaty palm still gripped her dagger and her whitened knuckles ached for relief.

They sat waiting for another five minutes, Avery guessed, before Moz sheathed his sword and finished crossing the river. He stepped right past them before stopping and turning on his heel to face them.

"We can slow the pace, but we keep moving forward. And I believe you have something of mine," he said to Avery pointedly.

Her eyebrows furrowed in confusion for a brief moment before she was struck with recollection. She set her rucksack down on the ground, crouching down on the ground to open the flap and Aegis immediately leaped out with Jack following. The rat scrambled forward into Moz's hand as he had bent down with an open palm on the ground.

"A moment longer and I might have eaten him."

Avery shrieked at the clarity of the voice now, falling backwards where she had been crouched. Aegis sat back on his haunches, tail swishing. Her eyes were widened with a combination of confusion and a fear of impending insanity.

"I... I think I have heat stroke, I thought I just heard my cat talking to me!" She laughed with nervousness, still leaning backwards on the ground. Moz raised a brow, placing the rodent on his shoulder.

"The cat?" Tristan asked, shrugging. "He's yer familiar, the Reapers all got 'em. Jack is Moz's guide."

Avery climbed up to her feet and looked down at Aegis. He had an attitude, for a cat at least, that he had to be around her at all times as though she would mess up horribly without him there.

"It sounds like he's talking in my head though, right there. Why couldn't I hear him before?"

Tristan was taking his hair out of its tie and shaking out the sweat. He stood back upright before answering her question.

"Did y'see the sigils painted on the wall of the city? I reckon it's a spell of some sort cast by either Morgana or one of her disciples. Not entirely sure what it does, but we think it dulls the Reapers. Ardua is Morgana's fortress in every sense of the word."

"And the people inside?"

"Either her subordinates or blissfully ignorant captives," Aegis' voice was smooth and from deep within the throat, much like his purrs when he was simply a housecat. She heard his answer much clearer than Tristan's and missed it entirely. She looked up at Moz and then Tristan for a reaction, but received nothing.

"Don't continue to seek out validation from them, only you can hear me."

But her focus remained on Tristan, who stood with arms folded now in observation. His stance was much more relaxed than before.

"So Aegis is just a cat that can talk? Do you realize how fucking crazy that sounds?" All of her questions were directed at the blonde giant, who was the one most willing to help. He shook his head.

"A demon," he clarified. "Nothin' to be alarmed by though. Just wary of. They were Yve's condition with th'other gods when she agreed to have death walk the soil. Familiars aren't evil, I reckon. Just tricky at times and it would be best to just get along."

Avery looked up at Moz, waiting for anything he had to add. Jack was balanced on his neck as he took off his black jacket. After he removed the right sleeve of the coat, she saw the black ink tattooed over his entire arm. It was hard to make out what the design was as he moved to shove the coat into his rucksack, but she thought she saw some form of a scaled creature around his bicep. When he looked back up with rolled tobacco in his mouth, he scowled at her and put the rucksack back on.

"Are we done with the pleasantries?" he jeered. "We don't have any time to sit around before it gets dark." He started forward, hacking away obstructing branches with a blade smaller than his white sword.

"I'll bring up the back, go on now Av'ry," Tristan shooed her forward.

Aegis was already bounding behind Moz without waiting for her. Avery grimaced in disapproval. All things considered, her current situation wouldn't be too awful if Moz wasn't so sour. She quickly stuffed her leather coat into her own sack and rushed to catch up.

The path Moz carved out sent them down rocky terrains and overgrown ferns. Avery did her best to follow closely, but her gaze often travelled upwards towards the leafy canopy before Tristan would scold her to keep focus. The forest around her buzzed with life, and she found herself listening to the birds chirping and the wind rolling over the branches.

Despite the dry heat of the air around them, Avery felt a cool sensation in the center of her belly as though she had just inhaled the relief of icy air. Her nerve endings stretched out from her center after being cramped inside a small box within her. She was suddenly hyper-aware of the way her teeth had been clenched together. The dryness of her tongue as it longed for water, the pounding under her ear lobes aching in her skull. She noticed the shifting of soil under her boots, the movement of her throat as she swallowed, and the way her fingers lightly swam through the air as her arms swung with movement.

Avery knew she should have felt overwhelmed but the awareness was comforting. Her jaw loosened and her pace picked up, a newfound bounce in her step.

They carried on for hours. Occasionally the roar of the river would rush to meet them again or whisper around them in the form of an off-shooting creek. They came across a small creek nestled between large, smooth rocks.

"This looks like the place to stop for a drink," Tristan confirmed and stooped down, opening a flask to fill it. Avery frowned at the water that rose to her ankles, as she had assumed they would push on even further. Moz had shown no signs of stopping, and was already on the opposite side of the creek. He had stopped, one leg up on a flat rock as though he was already wanting to leave.

"Not for too long. We can still travel further before we have to make a camp."

Avery looked at the water cautiously. Her feet were already soaked and raw, and yet the cold felt heavenly on her aches. The water was clear as ice, the smooth stones visible in the shallow water. She looked at Aegis lapping at it from the bank where Tristan stood. The demon did seem to know a lot more than she did, so certainly it was safe to drink here. She uncapped her empty bottle and dipped it into the water, the current making a satisfying gurgle as it filled the container.

She couldn't seem to drink the water fast enough to satisfy her thirst, the aches of dehydration were already dulling as her throat iced over with relief. After drinking to the bottom for a second time, she filled up the container once more and returned it to her rucksack. Avery opened her mouth to call out to Tristan, but she was interrupted by a crashing of branches from everywhere around them.

Moz already had his sword withdrawn before she had even looked over at him, Tristan unsheathing his own but slightly clumsier than his partner. Avery reached into her pocket where she had uncomfortably stashed her loaned dagger. The forest around them fell quiet aside from the movement of the water and wind running through the branches. Aegis stood rigid with alertness, watching the trees. She paced backwards a few steps before spinning around to pick the cat up.

"Tristan?" When she called out, she was hesitant to speak loudly, afraid of who or what her voice may be echoing to. The men were acting differently than when a deer or bird had crossed their path; they were anticipating something far worse.

Tristan was facing forward as Moz was, but momentarily cocked an ear in her direction to silently signal he was listening. Avery noted the silent gesture and softened her voice.

"Why was it that the police wouldn't follow us here? Neither of you have even told me yet, I have been asking and it…" she trailed off as she watched Moz on the opposite bank as he crouched low and disappeared into the brush.

"I'm sorry we haven't given you the answers, Avery," Tristan murmured while watching the brush Moz ducked into. "We're not entirely sure why, but the forest here is attractin' a lot of of spirits. Some demons. It's not really a problem during the day, but come nightfall y' need to really be alert." He turned and surveyed the bank behind them with an once-over glance, before looking at her.

"I promise, we'll fill y' in as soon as we're somewhere safe. Just this escape takes priority, we're only mostly sure the goons won't follow."

She nodded, accepting his explanation. As they waited for Moz to re-emerge, the wind rustling through the trees seemed louder than before. An illusion of sound, she thought. Now that she knew they definitely were not alone in this forest, the pricking of eyes burned holes in her skin, yet when she whirled in different directions she saw no one. Nothing? Avery wasn't sure what she had been expecting to find.

"You're responding to them, and they're responding to you now", Aegis purred from within her looped arm.

She looked down at the cat expecting the glassy stare, but he watched the trees as well with twitching whiskers and pupils the size of the moon. Avery bent her head a little lower to respond, not entirely comfortable yet with the idea of talking to her cat.

"What do you mean?" She whispered. His chest vibrated under her fingers, laughing throatily.

"Everything here has life. The trees have felt you and carry your vibrations through the roots to everything else. Of course, they're benign. They can feel your awareness now and they await to see your response so the others can pounce. You need to always be ready."

Avery's hand tightened around the dagger, almost as tight as her lungs felt. Pounce? She thought they were safe away from the city. It was impossible to keep every direction in her sights, to account for every single snap of a twig in the forest. Gods help her if she died of a heart attack over a creeping squirrel.

"I don't know anything about fighting," she hissed quietly to Aegis. His throat vibrated even more with an assumed laughter.

"You think I don't know that? You thought it was an accomplishment to simply go outside after dusk." She frowned at his words, but didn't protest as he continued, *"In reality, you only know nothing because that was my mistress' intent. You're still awakening from being within the sigils. When the time comes, you'll know what to do."*

"Your mistress?"

The cat looked back at her, his eyes serious and his small body was rigid.

"Don't you forget where I come from."

The Beldam. Avery looked at him warily before looking up to see Tristan was climbing up the bank to follow Moz. Her grip loosened around Aegis as though somehow touching him had put her in danger, but she continued to hold him as she trudged through the creek to follow the men.

Ultimately the cat was to serve the underworld; he had said so himself. Was Aegis the enemy too? After all, being a demon meant to serve the Beldam who was creeping into every crevice of the earth. She knew she had to eliminate any threat to Lily, to everyone else left in the city. Avery's heart ached thinking of her friend.

Yet Moz also kept a demon by his side. Surely Moz, who seemed bent on destroying this evil, would have left Jack behind if the rat was a threat to his cause. Or was Moz even to be trusted? Avery's paused as she considered this. Surely trustworthy people did not take others by force.

The gaze from the invisible eyes dug deeper into her back, making her even more nervous that she knew it was not just in her imagination. She preferred the feeling before Aegis confirmed the presence of the spirits.

The sound of Tristan hacking at branches brought her back to the present and she knew that it was too late for doubts. She couldn't simply turn back to Ardua. She climbed the bank to see the men standing several yards away, both of their weapons lowered. Tristan's head was tilted downward and Moz crouched low toward the ground. Avery drew nearer to see what they were gazing at.

The girl's blonde hair was splayed about her head on the ground beneath her, and she looked up at them with foggy eyes that never blinked during the long silence. Her mouth was agape with an unfinished scream. Avery's horrified gaze travelled down and she couldn't help but retch.

Congealed blood covered what was left of the young woman's throat, the flesh was ripped into gory ribbons by some kind of an animal. Swords were too clean for that.

The beginning of sour decay curled around Avery's nostrils and she vomited behind the tree once more. The scent of gore made her head spin and she stumbled to regain her sense of balance as she wiped her mouth.

Turning around, she caught a glimpse of Moz lifting one of her hands, turning it over as much as the full rigor mortis would allow. The bottom of her rigid hands were a dark purple where the blood had been pooling for quite some time.

"I reckon she's been dead for about twelve hours. What was the girl doing out here alone?" Tristan muttered.

He shook his head sympathetically. Moz, however, didn't reflect this sentiment and it itched at

Avery's growing disgust with him. He crouched, balancing on his toes, and he pinched the bridge of his nose between his thumb and pointer finger. Avery saw his eyes suddenly widen, and he shot up again with his sword re-drawn. Tristan only lifted his halfway in confusion.

"What's the matter?"

"There isn't a drop of blood at all on the ground beneath her," Moz observed with a bleak tone. "Even with the cleanest of cuts, there would be some spill. But an animal?"

Avery covered her mouth and nose with the collar of her shirt to block out the smell as best as she could, and stepped forward to confirm this.

He was right. It was a miracle her head was still attached to her body, given how much flesh had been ripped from her neck, but there was no blood to be found on the earthly bed beneath her

"She was moved here by someone," she told the men with her voice muffled by her shirt.

Moz and Tristan were looking about, scanning the treetops. She didn't have to point out that there were no broken branches or flattened plants from dragging a body. The young woman was either carried very carefully or more likely dropped from above as they heard from the crash in the trees moments before.

"You're becoming sharper by the very second. I told you."

After he purred within her skull, she put Aegis inside her rucksack to maintain focus. The cat meowed in protest as she put the sack back on, gripping her dagger so it pointed in front of her. She opened her mouth to speak, but Moz raised a fist to shoulder height, signaling silence. They stood, hushed, for several minutes without even the gentlest breeze to create a rustling of leaves. The heavy quiet made Avery uneasy, and she rocked side to side on the balls of her feet from behind where Moz and Tristan stood still as statues.

Her eardrums could have split from the sudden loud roar that came out of nowhere. Moz dodged the mass that lurched at him from a blind spot in their path. When it missed its intended target, it crashed into the tree behind where he had been standing.

It looked at first to be a man, dressed in a heavy green jacket, pocketed black cargo pants, and a ripped orange shirt. His amber skin was coated in dirt, with splatters of blood across his hard cheeks. But it was his eyes that sent Avery's heart pounding. There was nothing in them, just black.

The man faced them, but black arms stemmed from his back. At the end of the shadowy limbs were claw-like hooks, two of them lodged in the bark of the tree to hold him upright. A black shadow peeked out from behind the man's curly brown hair, like a second head sprouting from behind his neck.

"POSSESSION!" Tristan boomed, echoing loudly off the trees around them.

The creature reacted with another roar, which came from the shadowed head rather than the man's mouth. As the shadow unhinged its jaws, Avery saw row after row of jagged teeth soiled with blood. The man's head turned from side to side, surveying with black eyes. Her eyes widened when it stopped on her and she was suddenly aware of how small her dagger was. Avery spun on her heels and ran in the opposite direction.

She crashed through the trees and almost immediately felt the beast upon her, catching up to her as if the distance between them had been only the length of a breath. Avery knew she didn't stand a chance with her back to the beast and she spun around with her blade in front of her, ready to swipe. The beast was closer than she had anticipated and she could have sworn her heart stopped before she was able to slash across the man's cheek. It stumbled backwards using two hooked legs, momentarily stunned before the demon opened its shark-like mouth and let out another blood chilling roar.

It swiped at her with the blunt side of the hook, sending her backwards into the ground and her dagger flew out of her hand. She screamed at the pain in the side of her torso, praying to the gods that one of the men would come to her aid now that she was defenseless. The possessed man skittered over to her, the human body lifted a few feet off the ground as it walked on its hooked legs.

Avery scaled backwards on her palms and feet, searching for her weapon while keeping her eyes fixed on the grotesque figure before her. She felt tears burn at her eyes as the beast grew closer and her hand was still empty by the time it was hovering over her.

The beast stooped low to sniff at its prey. The scent of decay wafted from the man's body as the demon came face to face with Avery. Rows of porcelain teeth grinned at her hungrily , and she felt her body drop as hope left her.

"Goddess, I-"

There was a ripping sound, and the world went red.

— ❦ —

Lily followed the man down the hall, her view obstructed by his wall-like frame. She wasn't sure that she was missing much, as the hallway was bleached white and interrupted only by the occasional black door.

"Officer Reese," the man passing them greeted and the officer ahead of her returned the nod. This carried on down the long hallway with every person they brushed by until they reached the door at the very end. He knocked on the door, then stood in a rigid pose as a sign of respect for whomever was about to answer.

"Reese." A woman greeted the officer. Her voice was warm and thick as spiced honey and the tenseness that had been gripping Lily's muscles eased slightly.

"I assume you have our witness? I do hope the dear isn't shaken too badly."

The officer stepped aside and Lily did her best not to reveal any hint of surprise at the source of the honey-soft voice she had just heard. The woman was at least fifteen years older than her, her frame thin as a rail. Pale skin stretched across gaunt features, making her smile and blue eyes seem harsher than they should have been. Her ginger hair was cut to her jaw in a bob, not a single strand fell out of place.

"Oh, come inside my office! You poor girl!" The woman put her hand on Lily's shoulder to guide her inside. Lily flinched at the touch but followed.

"I'm twenty-three," she had meant to say this pointedly, but it sounded more like a defeated whimper than a correction.

She was led into a dark office, its walls paneled in dark wood and the lush carpet a deep crimson that felt heavenly under Lily's aching heels. All that filled the room was an enormous desk, two simple chairs at the front of it and a luxe leather chair behind it. The windows provided only enough light to illuminate the room, the white gauze curtains softening the harsh view of Ardua below. The woman motioned for Lily to take a seat, a smile stretched across her face. Lily wiped tears off her cheeks once more and sat in one of the simple chairs as Reese closed the door behind them to stand at attention next to it.

"Officer, I--" she started, fumbling with her hands in her lap over the fabric of her blue dress.

"Please, you're not in trouble nor are you any of my subordinates. You can call me Morgana," the woman smiled, watching Lily with glassy eyes as she sat down in the leather chair before her. Lily felt uneasy and looked about the room, anywhere but Morgana's eyes.

"I understand you're feeling very shocked right now," she spoke in a warm tone. "But I will cut right to it, there's no point in dancing around the subject."

Morgana cleared her throat with a palm pressed flat on her sternum before folding her hands on the desk to continue. "The young woman you live with--"

"Avery Porter. And she's my sister," Lily interrupted. Over her dead body would she ever allow Avery to become a nameless victim. Lily was used to seeing the slight raise of the brow whenever she used the word to refer to Avery, but she never bothered to explain Avery's adoption into the Clements family.

"Yes, Miss Porter. Miss Porter was coerced by two men, a kidnapping of a certain kind. These two men have slain six of my officers in cold blood, you saw that for yourself. This isn't the first time they have killed either, as we have evidence linking them to murders in Brightloch as well as Centralia. We have reason to believe they're using Miss Porter as a human shield in order to commit an act of violence against the Crown." Her voice was slow now, the gravity of the situation evident.

Fear grabbed her by the throat and squeezed. Despite her hardest efforts more tears streamed down Lily's cheek. "Are... are they going to kill her too?"

Morgana stared at her for a moment, gathering the words to say and this pause only succeeded in making Lily's chest hurt with panic. What was going to happen to her dearest friend? Avery said herself she would be back, but how could she really know? They were just held at knifepoint by murderers who would probably have no problem killing again.

"There's a good chance they will simply release Miss Porter after succeeding. That is of course, under their assumption of succeeding. She has no connection to the Crown and nothing of value to offer. The fact that you were kept alive tells me they only kill when threatened or have reaped every benefit. I have no reason to believe they are threatened by or want anything from Miss Porter."

Lily began nodding slowly as she tried to force the relieving information to sink in. When it finally did, her fingers that had been knotted within each other unlaced and her head was still. Avery had guts and almost certainly she knew how to keep herself alive. The girl she knew was street-smart and knew how to throw a punch or two, or at least she did in high school. She had to believe that Avery would be okay.

"Which leads me to my proposal," Morgana continued. "Miss Porter may not be aware how easy her getaway would actually be. She is coming between us and the extermination of these murderers; swift extraction from the situation can and will save her life. We would like to send you westward to retrieve her. She is more likely to feel safer around a friend than she would with only an armed squad."

Lily's eyes widened. "You want me… to what?"

Morgana smiled. "We will arm you to our fullest capability, and we will ask you to help us retrieve your sister to remove her from harm."

Lily's eyebrow lifted up in suspicion. "But, won't that only just put me in danger instead? The use of civilians in police investigations has statistically proven to be…"

Her voice trailed off when she saw the smile on Morgana's face - the kind people wore as a way to hide their agitation.

"She's family, though… I'll go," she finished quietly. Morgana's smile stretched wide, and tilted her head to the side in an almost puppy-like way.

"You are very brave," she cooed and her honey-thick voice sent the smallest hairs on Lily's neck standing straight up. Patronizing bitch.

"I assure you, both you and Miss Porter will be just fine. You'll be guided and accompanied by only our finest! Now if you'll allow me to guide you to the arsenal and we'll have you on the first ship west."

CHAPTER THREE
THE HIGH PRIESTESS

Moz stood over the corpse before Tristan was even able to reach the possessed man. He had reached into his belt for blessed waters and tools from the Temple before he had even considered simply slaying the beast. Tristan wasn't given the chance to exorcise the man before he was dead.

Tristan stood over Avery. She was drenched in the blood of the man whose sliced body had been kicked over to her left side. Moz flicked his sword before sheathing it and stepped back. Her face should have been painted with terror but Tristan found no such expression on the girl. She simply laid on the earth, stunned and coated slick in someone else's blood.

Tristan put away his waters and knelt beside her to help her stand back up. While she was able to carry most of her own weight, there was something stiff about her movement now and any sign of the girl who had been whistling happily on the trail hours ago was long gone. The side of her white shirt bloomed red with blood where the demon had lashed at her.

"We'll fix y' right up Avery," he assured her and coaxed Avery into sitting on a fallen tree. Still her face held no expression but she complied without any questioning or arguing as she had before. From his rucksack, Tristan pulled a bottle of spirit he kept solely for medicine rather than for purposes of pleasure.

Ripping off part of the bottom hem of his shirt, he soaked it in the burning liquid. Before she could protest, he put a palm down on her shoulder to hold her still and pressed the wet fabric against the palm-sized wound under her ribcage. She howled in pain and part of Tristan was relieved that she had even reacted at all. He held the fabric in place for a moment, apologizing repeatedly but received no response. He looked up from the wound to see she had been biting her lower lip until her small chin turned red, presumably to prevent more cries.

"I know, I'm sorry," he said sympathetically and took the blood-soaked cloth away to store it in a small leather container. He knew it was best not to leave it laying in the dirt where the scent could be picked up and used for tracking. Tristan ripped the hem of his shirt again in a longer length to tie it around her waist for compression. He was able to tie it around twice before securing it.

"Keep it nice n' tight. It should hold up 'til we get to Centralia. Shank will fix ya right up."

He stood up, offering his arm for Avery to grip as she was slower to stand. She ignored the help and remained silent. Tristan whirled around looking for Moz to find him crouched where the attack had taken place, rubbing his temple once more. He frowned and folded his arms in agitation.

"I could have exorcised him y'know. All it would've taken was—"

"If I had let you do that, the girl would be dead," Moz argued flatly. He was clearly distracted by something in front of him, and Tristan stepped forward to see what had caught his eye. On the ground was a patch of mushrooms varying in size and color, some yellow pins and others red plates.

"What are y' lookin at? The mushrooms?"

Moz turned back to look at him, the scarred eyebrow lifted questioningly. "I didn't notice them before. Did you? They should have been obliterated either by her fall or the demon." He pointed to the blood in the soil.

Tristan frowned. Whether this was the work of Beldam or the Middle Sister, he did not know. Of all the demons he had slain or exorcised he couldn't recall the earth blooming where their blood had splattered. He looked over his shoulder at Avery, standing yards away with blood still smeared on her face. Her familiar paced around her ankles impatiently.

"I reckon we shouldn't worry," he advised. "Just keep an eye out for big-game demons who might do the same. Keep an eye on Ave, too."

Moz stood up, his spidery limbs straightening out in one fluid motion. His eyes remained down on the blooming fungi before speaking. "It will be dark soon. We need to make finding shelter our priority. You don't suppose Nora will be coming this far north, do you?"

Before Tristan could answer, Avery called in a tone almost as flat as Moz's. "Who's Nora?"

Moz had already turned and started continuing on their path. Tristan sighed, knowing he would be the one to explain once again. "Follow him, an' I'll tell you."

She looked at him with suspicion, but she turned around to follow Moz. He walked several steps behind her, his blade out, and he scanned around the area with caution as he spoke.

"Moz is a pretty old Reaper, probably one of the oldest still alive," he started. "In his time in Centralia, he befriended the daughter of a tradesman and his wife, who was a healer. Which isn't unheard of considering how long he's been floatin' around. He told me that as she grew older, Nora took up the practice of her mother doin' natural remedies and healing. She was fairly successful and took over the practice after her mother died. How did she die?"

"Childbirth," Moz filled in without missing a beat and Tristan nodded his head, remembering more of the details now.

"She died in childbirth after givin' birth to the fourth son," he continued, watching Avery's shoulders for a moment before scanning again.

"Nora took over the practice. I reckon she had been feeling pretty overwhelmed, her skills were far superior to anyone the village had access to. Anyway, somewhere her practice took a turn fer th' worst. She began to consult the dead for healing, resortin' to blood work, and all kinds of things having to do with the work of Beldam. She became known as the Witch of Centralia."

"When word of her craft reached the devout tradesman, he personally dragged her in for persecution. The villagers hung her at the edge of the forest, and she was there 'til her bones were picked bare. After I met Mr. Mosley there, we encountered her spirit at the woods. I swear to you, she was the most intelligent but malevolent spirit I've encountered to this day. Full-bodied apparition. I think we're too far north. I reckon she doesn't travel this far."

He nearly stumbled over Avery when she had slowed, his swiveling gaze missing the sudden change of pace.

"I'm sorry about your friend, Moz," she whispered. Tristan could not see her face but the sympathy was tangible in her sudden softness.

His partner looked over his shoulder back at them as he walked and Tristan expected the signature scowl. When it was absent he felt a nearly-physical jolt in his frame seeing the emptiness in Moz's face. He said nothing to the girl, returning his attention forward and never stopping his pace.

The silence that followed was initially uncomfortable and he wasn't sure if he should continue trying to talk about Nora with a happier tone. He had only known the young woman through the stories told about her. Tristan decided that silence would be much better.

They walked for quite some time and he spent much of it noticing the curled ends of Avery's hair bouncing as she stepped, like the locks of a child. His child. Helena and Aubrey had been gone for quite some time, but in moments like these Tristan found a sick desire to pour salt in his wounds again.

Helena. Tristan was too ashamed to admit even to Moz that there have been times he had nearly allowed a demon to slay him, anything to bring him back to his wife. Now here Avery was, and he saw so much of their Aubrey in her. He would have given anything to see his little girl grow to this age.

It was her that broke the heavy silence. "Will you tell me everything now, Tristan?"

She didn't turn around or even glance behind her as she spoke; there was no trace of desperation in her request as there had been earlier that day. Still he nodded even though she couldn't see him.

"Aye, I did promise that. We must keep forward though, keep the pace."

As they kept walking with Moz in the lead, Tristan began to explain.

"Like I told you last night, Beldam offered the Reapers up as a solution to the imbalance a perfect humanity would have brought. Both the goddesses Ara and Yve were fooled by this illusion, with the hope that Beldam was sincere. You an' I both know she wasn't, because here we are."

"She began to hide her own demonic entities, known as the Knights of Od, within the Reapers. She forged them in the fires of her underworld with the help of Paion, the god of war. Morgana was the first Knight to be created. These Knights hold domain over the elements: water, fire, earth, an' wind. The fifth and final Knight occupies spirit. Moz an' I got word from the High Priestess of Centralia that the last Knight woke. All o' the Beldam's pawns are in place. That's why Morgana is making her move and we're gonna in'ercept them before she does. The High Priestess told us to go to Ardua for a companion, and I reckon she meant you....'

"Anyway, now that we've collected you, we gotta gather our companions waiting fer us in Centralia. We go from there after the Priestess tells us where the final Knight is."

He almost expected Avery to demand to hear the rest of the information, as though she knew he was withholding something. Moz's face certainly showed it as he glanced over his shoulder and looked at Tristan with a criticizing glare.

"Avery, stop here for a drink. I need to speak with Tristan."

Moz walked ahead a few more yards so that they would be out of earshot, and Tristan followed with glances over his shoulder at Avery to make sure she was distracted. She drank from her container without seeming quizzical at all, but Aegis glared at the men from between her booted ankles.

"So you're just going to omit a huge piece of information, huh," Moz accused.

He looked up at Tristan with anger. Tristan let out a loud sigh of frustration before realizing he was supposed to be quiet.

"I reckon telling you all hasn't proven to be helpful," he muttered. "If I tell her that she's supposed to be looking for a missing emotion, she'll pressure herself into finding it. Ya' can't find it sincerely that way… You haven't found it, and you're the oldest of all of us. Maria hasn't found it, Shank hasn't found it… maybe the kid has a chance if she isn't looking."

Moz's jaw visibly clenched with anger and unsettled Tristan. He knew he was the biggest of the pair, but he still felt the fear of Od burn in him when he saw that muscle move.

"I know you're only here to do your holy work," Moz spoke coldly. "And I know you're aware that no matter what happens to any of us, you're still Saved. Bless your fuckin' soul. But I think any of us, even that kid over there, deserves to know we can be in the same graces as a priest if we can find the capacity to feel something… something that demon whore thought would be fuckin' hilarious to leave out."

Tristan opened his mouth to speak, but the frustration he'd felt in his friend's voice had left him rattled and he closed it again. He expected Moz to stalk off but he did no such thing. Instead he glared at Tristan with such contempt that he became aware that this wasn't just about telling Avery about the emotion clause.

When Reapers became capable of experiencing a particular emotion they'd been created without, they became Saved. Relieved of their duties and guaranteed paradise. Tristan had only known of one Reaper who was Saved and he would do anything to ensure his friends were Saved as well.

"I know you resent me, William," Tristan dared to use his first name as he wasn't sure how else to convey how serious he was. "But I beg ya, let's keep that bit mum… I reckon she won't find her hidden emotion if she's lookin' for it. If she doesn't find it within three months, I'll tell her. I'll get the Priestess to tell her if I have to."

Moz looked at him for a long moment with the same stare and Tristan expected the man to lash out at him. Instead, he turned around to walk away in frustration and he heard him huff in annoyance, "Damn straight."

"We stop here for the night."

Moz came to a halt, and Avery slammed into his back, as she had been following him closely while watching the black orbs return from the shadows of the trees. Though she knew that these orbs posed no threat, she couldn't help but search for the white eyes beyond them that belonged to the humanoid shadows.

"Will the Leeches be a problem out here?" she asked Moz, calling the demons by their name that he had spat before in disgust.

They had stopped in a small ring of trees, the stars peeking from the small spaces left between their canopies. Moz drew his blade and dropped his rucksack on the ground. Jack crawled out of the opening, and scurried across the forest floor toward Aegis.

"Not as much," he mumbled flatly and Avery let out a small groan of frustration at his overall apathy. "Since there's no foot traffic through this part of the woods, there's nothing for them to feed on. Which is both good and bad…"

Avery watched as he began dragging his sword on the ground behind him, her forehead scrunched in confusion. He walked in a large circle, trailing around the large oak behind where she stood and made a five foot radius around it. Moz stopped and looked at the broken soil before a slight look of satisfaction came over his face that she would have missed had she not been watching him so closely. He then called out to Tristan.

"Circle's done, do your stuff," after sheathing his sword, he continued addressing her concern.

"The small ones don't pose too much of a threat, but they are desperate and will pick up on any hint of panic or despair in you. That means we have to be far warier of them than in Ardua, where they had plenty to feast upon… why are you making that face?"

Avery tried to stifle her laughter halfway through his explanation, but stopped as soon as he mentioned it. "I'm sorry, I didn't think you could talk so much!"

He scowled at her, mumbling something under his breath before turning away.

After he stalked off, Avery whirled around to see Tristan kneeling at the inner edge of the circle. He had pulled out several vials earlier when the possessed man attacked, and now they were on the ground before him where he sat at the line Moz had drawn. His face was skyward and he held his hands together while mumbling words Avery couldn't understand. She sat down silently at the base of the tree a modest distance away from Tristan so she could watch.

He poured the liquid contents of a translucent purple vial into a green one, his movements made with utmost care and caution. Setting them down, he pressed his forehead to the dirt in a bow with his hands cupped around his knees. For a brief moment, Avery felt the earth around her sigh with wind and the chatter of birds crescendo before disappearing all at once. She didn't realize how loud the sound had been until her eardrums throbbed, trying to make up for the sudden silence. Before she had time to comment on the phenomenon, Tristan sat upright again and stood up, the vials collected in his hands.

"Make sure everyone is within the circle. Aegis, Jack, and Moz."

She nodded even though he would not have been able to see. Avery surveyed her side of the tree, but there was no sign of the small cat nor of the rat. "Aegis?" she called out.

"We already know how this works," the feline emerged from behind the tree, Jack standing upright behind him and looking up at her with beaded ebony eyes. Avery crouched on one knee to level with the demonic pair.

"Did you see where Moz went?"

Aegis had raised his front paw halfway to his small mouth to lick it clean, but put it back down as he looked at her. The cat then peered behind his left side at Jack.

"Where has your Master gone?" Avery was able to hear Aegis pose the question in a low purr, but her lack of connection to Jack left her without an answer. Upon realizing the ridiculousness of being frustrated she couldn't communicate with the rat, she chuckled. When Aegis turned back to her, she was met with a glare hot with annoyance.

"*Up*," was all he said.

"W-what? That doesn't tell me, oh," she looked up inside the treetops of the oak from the ground.

The height was so dizzying that she sat down in order to focus her eyes better. Initially, it looked as though all she was staring at was a dark canopy of leaves casting the limbs of the great tree in shadows. On a branch fifteen feet above the soil she caught sight of a pair of scuffed black boots, noticing them only from their quick movement across the thick branch. Moz was visible when a square of light came across his hardened face before he vanished as quickly as he had appeared.

Avery used her hands to push herself upright and she returned to Tristan. He was pouring the clear contents of the green container into the tiny moat Moz had carved out with his sword. With careful movements, his feet shuffled along the inside of the circle as he trailed the liquid into the dirt.

"Aegis and Jack are inside… and Moz is in the tree," she said slowly to Tristan, trying not to startle him as he focused. He chuckled in a staccato manner, then sharply fell silent as he buried himself in focus again.

She waited for two long minutes before receiving a response.

"Moz always takes it upon 'imself to be the sentinel," he explained. "You won't be seein' much o'him for the rest of the night. Go rest."

Avery huffed, annoyed by being bossed around by the exorcist but still took off her rucksack with a careless drop to the ground. She sat with her back against the coarse bark of the oak and her knees pulled upward to her chest.

Shadowed anomalies continued to appear in the brush around them, their accumulating presence made startlingly clear by white eyes that watched her. They didn't seem to be attached to bodies. The eyes of the forest Avery had felt earlier that day as they had crossed the river had made themselves known. They belonged to the trees, to the brush, to the fallen timber.

As night fell into its peak darkness, the murmuring of the forest kindred grew to a dull roar. Avery's eyes drooped heavy with sleepiness but she refused to shut them for even a moment as she watched the elongated shadow float just outside the circle. The giant eel-like demon soared upwards towards the sky and bobbed back down again in a slow repetition, circling them for the dozenth time. No matter where the creature was around the circle, Avery was convinced its empty white eyes were fixated on her. It was waiting just outside the edge of the circle to strike. Going to sleep wasn't an option, even though Tristan had personally guaranteed that the circle would hold.

Several small knives were lodged in the soil in front of them. While the circle had been drawn, there were still forest demons occupying the great tree where they had made their base and had become trapped inside. Moz was still high above the ground sitting sentry and had sent his blades to the ground like spears, the demons spilling black ooze as their incorporeal forms were somehow pierced. Avery still didn't understand how.

"You're goin' to need sleep eventually," Tristan chided without warning and Avery seized up in fright with her white knuckles gripped around her knees. She had refused to move for hours and her muscles buzzed with static. There was a heavy pressure pulling her top eyelids down as though to beg for sleep. While her eyes were fixated forward to watch the floating form she saw

Tristan reaching into his rucksack through her peripheral vision. He sighed in exasperation.

"Don't hate me for this, Ave."

He held an open vial under her nostrils and before she could realize what was happening, she inhaled a bitter scent. Clouds rolled in from the sides of her head and fogged over her heavy eyes. Before she was able to demand an explanation, the world turned sideways and then black.

– ✦ –

There was nothing around her but grass, giving slightly under the weight of her bare feet. Looking down, it was mere shades away from the cotton gown draped around Avery. Dark grey clouds above her head rolled low to the ground with a speed that was beyond compare of other formations she had seen in her life. She turned around, the spin of her limbs feeling weighed down.

The hills behind her rolled like water, all of them covered in the same lush blanket of grass. There was not a tree, nor river, nor village to be seen; just a giant curled in a green sleep. Humidity beaded on her furrowed brow as she frowned. Where on earth was she? She whirled back around and the scenery changed.

She stood before a wrought-iron gate towering eight feet above her head. Circles and lines and meaningless shapes were woven into the vertical bars. Sigils? What are sigils? Somebody had mentioned them to her, but who?

Avery looked to her left and saw that the iron fence never seemed to end, expanding way beyond her horizon's vanishing point. To her right was the same. The gate itself was shut in front of her, adorned with purple and green jewels at its top with intricate spirals reaching down to the damp earth. The feeling of curiosity as to why she was there weighed on her head, but no words could be formed in her skull nor on her tongue. Between the iron stems of the fence she saw nothing but grass. Why was a gate here? Why around nothing?

A crow cawed above her from its perch on the gate, its feet wrapped around a deep violet stone. She flinched in surprise and she looked up at the iridescent bird. The crow was much larger than ones she had seen in... where? She couldn't remember, but she knew that the black birds were not supposed to be as tall as her. Avery knew she should have been afraid, but she wasn't. Instead she looked back down in front of her, her fingers trying to pry the unlocked gate open. The metal refused to move.

"You think you can just dance into my home?" the crow cawed, its shrill voice filling the air for miles. She looked up, the corvid's beady eyes reflecting her gaze back at her. Her own reflection shifted faces, her hair moving from blonde to auburn and her jaw warped and she could not remember what she was supposed to look like.

"You think you can just dance into my home without asking?" the crow cawed again. Avery was not sure if it demanded an answer, but she was unable to open her mouth to form a response. She felt frustration gnaw from the inside of her stomach as she was made aware of her forced silence. Searching the ground, she began looking for a small stone to throw at the bird. As her fingers closed around small pebbles, they melted into mud and dripped to the ground.

"You think you can just dance into my home without asking? And without any offering?" the bird

repeated once more and again Avery bent to pick up pebbles.

The stones she grasped fell to the ground, this time becoming reflective coins when they hit the grass. Avery picked them up, turning them in her hand. There were no seals on them, though she wasn't quite sure what those were supposed to look like. Without questioning what she was doing, she placed the three coins on the ground at the foot of the iron doors in a triangular form. Why was she doing this?

The crow cackled. "You did bring an offering! Ask the gatekeeper once more!"

Who was the gatekeeper? Maybe whoever they were, they were listening. Avery was finally able to open her mouth to speak. She felt her jaw and tongue move properly, but her ears heard a muffled mumble as though she were listening to a voice underwater. Whatever she said must have been right, for the crow cackled with laughter once more.

"Now we're getting somewhere!"

The crow flapped its wings, hitting Avery's face with a sharp wind as it took off into the sky. The gates in front of her opened on their own accord with a shrill creak of metal. Although it had appeared the fence held nothing behind it when she had first peeked inside, a graveyard was suddenly sprawled before her. The clouds above it were gloomier, and bubbling puddles pooled in the muddy footpaths.

She looked behind her at the sleepy grass hills and back before her. It seemed she straddled the line between two different worlds. Avery stepped forward into the graveyard and the iron doors shut slowly behind her.

Cracking leaves fell to the ground with slow grace as she stepped forward. The wings of the large bird unsettled the air around the vast estate of the dead but its dark iridescence was nowhere to be seen. She followed the sound down a muddy pathway but never felt the earthly ooze accumulating on the skin of her feet. Avery looked around the graveyard, peering between mausoleums, stone lambs, and marble urns. The bird of titanic proportions was nowhere to be found.

She considered turning back to the gate, but her feet kept trudging forward of their own volition. The flapping of wings had disappeared, leaving the graveyard in a heavy silence. Avery almost wished one of its residents would emerge and direct her to an exit. She felt a laugh bubble in the pit of her throat at the thought but the sound failed to escape her. The closer she traveled to the center of the graveyard, the darker it grew. Not from the fog nor from the clouds, but as though her vision was beginning to fail her.

The crow screamed from behind her, and she was finally able to cry out in surprise as she fell into the mud. She looked over her shoulder as she rose onto her palms and knees to get up, seeing the giant bird perched on top of a spherical stone grave marker.

"Are you afraid?" The crow spoke this time without the harsh caw.

Avery had climbed to her feet, her gown weighed down by the mud that clung to her. She wiped hair out of her face and looked at the bird. It stared back with a curious gaze and its large head cocked to the left as it waited for a response. She wondered if she was able to fit in its large beak and be swallowed whole - surely birds ate young women like her.

"No."

She had barely finished the single word before the bird cackled with laughter, throwing its head back.

"You can't lie to me!"

"I am afraid," she found herself saying immediately despite her original intent to become silent. The feathered beast returned its glare to her with serious eyes.

"I understand that you are fleeting and a mere blink. But your fear is not necessary here. Your domain reaches much further than you thought," the crow declared.

Avery was puzzled. She felt a question sitting on her tongue, but the ever-annoying force she felt still prevented her from speaking. It wasn't until then she noticed the white, misty forms emerging from the soil around them. Humanoid shapes crawled out from the ground before the grave markers, featureless and void of any substance. Her mouth opened to scream but there was only a raspy exhale as her lungs failed her. From her throat emerged a papery substance, foreign to her at first. She held open her hands as she spit out the object. A marigold the color of the summer sun sat in her open palm, still dry despite the wetness of her mouth.

The crow only watched her in silence as she coughed up another marigold, loose petals fluttering to the mud at her feet. Instead of approaching the girl and the giant corvid, the white figures stood in a circle around them, the nearest of them ten feet away from Avery. She was soon pulling handfuls of marigolds out of her mouth. A bouquet's worth of the flowers sat at her feet before her front lobe ached with a searing pain.

Stems emerged from the pores of her forehead and quickly they blossomed into more of the golden flowers. Marigolds bloomed above her eyebrows, petals shedding as they grew in size. A scream escaped her throat, shrill with fear. The flowers began to fringe on her field of vision and the crow threw its head back once more in a harsh laughter.

"Do not be afraid," it said and repeated "Your domain reaches much further than you thought."

Her scream was stifled when her mouth filled to the brim of her lips with petals and her vision was taken over by a gold sheet of silken flowers.

CHAPTER FOUR
THE EMPRESS

Morgana threw herself upright from where she laid in her captain's chamber. Sweat soaked her skin and had turned her nightgown into suffocating rags. She kicked the heavy blanket off her legs, bending as far forward as she could to see them in the pitch dark to reassure herself that her limbs were still attached. Slowly her eyes adjusted and the pale flesh came back into view in the moonlight pouring in through the portholes behind her bed. The black serpents and comforting flame that resided permanently in the flesh of her left leg wobbled back into focus.

"It's a dream… just a dream," she mumbled to herself, in desperation to comfort herself when no one else could.

Being buried alive, burning at the stake, drowning, the earth swallowing her whole. These were just a few highlights of the dreams she had ever since the last Knight came into play. She knew it was no coincidence; this was Beldam giving her an incentive to finish. To pay her debt.

She fumbled in the dark as she walked to a writing desk at the opposite end of the chamber, knowing she had left her lighter and cigarettes on top of it. It took her two tries to ignite a flame and felt a faint glow of relief in her chest when she sucked the smoke inward. Morgana used the same lighter to ignite an oil lantern and immediately wished she hadn't when she saw her own reflection.

Worry was heavy on her lower lids and she knew it only grew when her gaze traveled down to bottom of the mirror where a photograph was wedged into the corner of the wood frame. The young woman smiled back at her, red hair as ablaze as her own. Morgana's heart ached for her daughter.

Where was Sera at that moment? She sucked in the tobacco in every effort to smoke out her paranoia. Hypothetical images of her sweet girl lying face down in a riverbed or strung high in a tree flashed in her mind; tears burned at the edges of her eyelashes before she wiped them away. Beldam had lied to her, they still had the chance to die and Morgana was hyper-aware of that fact at every waking moment.

"Was it worth the sacrifice?"

So then the demon was awake, too. Or did it ever sleep? She didn't shrug the Knight off this time; they got along mostly, aside from the occasional inopportune remarks. If it would keep her from falling asleep again, she would entertain the query.

"Of course it was worth it. Henry is gone, but Sera is still here. She's all I need."

"Quite impressive, if you think about it. No Soul before her had skipped death and went straight to Reaping. Beyond that, even. But you haven't escaped death just yet, little flame."

"She knew I wouldn't have done it if Sera wasn't included," she stamped her cigarette out on a metal tray and climbed back into her bed. She sat upright in a blurry daze with the blanket pulled up to her waist.

"It was my fault anyway. I knew Henry was going to die, that was only a matter of when. My child was more important to me than a fleeting love, I couldn't imagine living in the new world without her."

—❦—

When Avery's eyes opened the forest was already illuminated by soft, early sunlight. Momentarily disoriented from her sideways position, she loosened her grip on the dirt she clenched in her left fist. Her rucksack that she had been leaning against the night before had somehow traveled yards away from where she was, her notebook and a leg of her spare jeans poking out of the opening. She sat upright and the inside of her skull felt like a snowglobe that had been turned upside down, its contents being shaken rapidly.

Any signs of the forest-dwelling demons were gone, leaving behind the conversations of birds above their heads and the warm kiss of the sun through the gaps in the leafy canopy. Aegis remained sleeping against her rucksack. Jack had already made a habit of keeping close to him, but the rat was nowhere to be seen. She stood up, brushing dirt off her clothes despite their blood-soaked state.

Moz was the first of the men Avery saw, his back was towards her and he waited outside where the circle stood. With the rare moment of stillness in him, she was finally able to make out the ink design that adorned his right arm. The scaled wings of a beast around his bicep appearing in a clouded sky, its head appeared close to that of a horse long past the first stage of decay. Around his forearm was a three-masted ship on a tumultuous sea, the skin above his wrist almost completely black for the pit of an ocean before cutting off at a clean line as to not impede on the back of his hand. She tried to make out more details of the artwork before Jack, who was perched on his right shoulder, glanced back at her with beady eyes and turned to say something to Moz.

Moz turned around and looked at Avery, his marred eyebrow raised. "Did you know that you're quite possibly the world's most violent sleeper?"

She scrunched her face with anger, her face growing hot.

"Fuck off."

He let out a sincere laugh, unlike the one she heard from him during the standoff at the river.

"You chucked your bag clear across the ring while you were asleep, nearly squashed your damn cat, and threw a bloody fit."

Her mouth opened as she prepared to fling back an insult when memory struck her. "Tristan…"

Avery stalked in the other direction to find the exorcist, the veins in her forehead throbbing with rage. He was found on the opposite side of the tree, filling the miniature moat they had made the night before in the dirt circle. Before approaching him, Avery grabbed the nearest loose stick and swatted at him. The branch wasn't heavy enough to cause genuine harm but he dropped his own stick and backed away in surprise, hands held up in front of his face.

"OW! What, are… you doin!"

She swatted him again in the stomach. "What am I doing? What were you doing? You drugged me!"

"It was an inhalant t'sleep! You were panicking an'- would ya' put the stick down?"

She felt angered steam emanating from the top of her head and her brow was still scrunched with rage, but she threw the stick down on the ground at her feet - only after swatting him once more. Avery folded her arms to make it clear she expected an explanation.

"Those were nothing but herbs I got from one of the people we're headin' back to… you were in such a panic and might have gone into shock. If I hadn't done that, you wouldn't be coherent at all right now and in bad shape… it was only to help."

Avery's frown remained. Despite his good intentions, she still felt enraged. She wasn't sure if she was most angry with the fact Tristan used it upon her or by the mere idea that such a mixture existed with that kind of power over someone.

"Regardless of your intentions… you still acted without asking. If you ever do that again, we're going to have a serious fucking problem," she said with a snarled lip and he visibly winced at the profanity.

Instead of waiting for an answer, she went back to Aegis and her rucksack to let him finish erasing the circle. Aegis stirred before she even reached him, woken from the sounds of her stomping - a little louder than what would be considered reasonable for a young adult. He sat back on his haunches and looked up at her as she swung the rucksack onto her back.

"Something's off."

"Yeah, well Tristan thought drugging me to avoid a panic would-"she huffed before the demon cut her off.

"No, not that. I'm not sure what it is… but it's certainly not that."

What could have been off if Aegis was unsure? She opened her mouth to pose the question, but fell silent when Moz approached them. It might have been best to keep the observation between the two of them, Avery wasn't sure yet how much she trusted Moz and the rat. She tried to ignore them for as long as possible and made herself more preoccupied with putting on her rucksack than it required.

"All closed, let's leave," she jumped in surprise when it was Tristan's voice who spoke behind her instead of Moz, who had rolled tobacco flickering between his teeth.

Tristan walked past her without a word and Moz fell into line in front of him as they had become accustomed to. She trailed behind Tristan as she put her hand against the pocket to reassure herself that the dagger, her only weapon, was still there. Though she couldn't have missed its bulky and uncomfortable form, it was different feeling it gripped in her hand through the denim fabric.

Tristan had claimed she was with the men serving as a companion, as predicted by the Priestess. Yet the feeling that she remained captive still hung over her head. They had seemed less concerned with keeping an eye on her the further into the forest they moved, but that was to be expected. Where would she run to if she decided to flee? Certainly not back to Ardua.

They trudged through the brush and branches until the high sun of noon inspired sweat on their foreheads when Aegis suddenly stopped. She nearly tripped over him and into Moz, as she had somehow ended up in the middle during their trek.

"Aegis, what's the matter?"

His small head was lifted as though to sniff the air, translucent whiskers twitching.

"I've figured it out. Somebody has been watching us," he purred.

Her gaze shifted from the cat to the trees to her left, though nothing seemed out of the ordinary. When she looked up, Moz had turned around and looked down at Aegis with a questioning glance.

"Somebody's watching us, he said," she relayed the information to them before looking back down at Aegis. "I thought the whole forest was watching? That's what you said yesterday."

"This is different. When the forest watches, it's a collective gaze from the spirits within. This is beside that."

"That makes no sense at all."

He circled around her feet, ignoring her remark, before trotting ahead of Moz. *"We need to keep moving, faster if we can."*

They followed the cat, Moz taking a long stride to fall back into his position as leader and shot a glance down at Aegis as he passed him. Avery frowned at the bizarre display between the two; Moz must not have been a fan of cats, she assumed.

"Who do you think is watching," she continued the seemingly one-sided conversation as she followed.

"Don't you think I would have told you if I knew? You're very impatient. It doesn't suit you."

Avery fumed. Why should she take the concern lightly? Demons were a little more durable than she had proven to be and it was her life possibly on the line, not his.

"It's substantially different than the earth-roaming demons, so whoever it is has an identity. Someone who's beyond being a familiar or bobbing sprite. That can be good or bad. I just do not recognize it."

They travelled in silence for two long hours and somehow Moz seemed even more on edge than he did as they left the riverbank. He took Aegis' note seriously and raised up his sword at every twig snap and flap of wings. She wondered if Moz would have flinched at a falling leaf had he paid attention to one.

"This definitely shouldn't be here," Moz said in a low voice as they stepped between the trees into a clearing. Beneath their feet was lush grass, tall and tickling the skin at the top of her boots. The men were talking in astonishment at their discovery but Avery couldn't hear them over her racing heartbeat.

Across the meadow stood an iron fence thirty yards wide. Panic flooded her as she recalled the massive gates from her dream. Her feet began to step on their own, drawing her in towards it. She willed herself to stop, digging her nails into her thigh but she kept pushing forward.

"What is that?" She heard Tristan behind her; she hoped she could somehow anchor herself to the sound. Whatever was drawing her in was much more powerful than her, and with a feeling near relief she decided that fighting it was futile. Aegis laughed with a strange heartiness in her head.

"I should have recognized it. I'm nearly certain we have nothing to fear," he purred as he bounded past her towards the gate.

"Nearly?"

Yet she followed Aegis to the gate where he waited for her, pacing in circles at its iron feet. She approached the fence, looking in at the graveyard. While it was densely populated, it was nowhere near the size of the sprawling cemetery from her dream. Seeing the doors were unlocked, she looked up.

Muddied circles of amethyst and emerald adorned the metal circles wrought into the iron, and the familiarity of it took the air out of her lungs. She turned to look at the men for any explanation. Moz had approached the gate with an expression that held no hint of alarm, maybe even familiarity. Tristan, on the other hand, was several yards behind them at a distance.

"Why are you all the way back there?" She asked. "You can see inside that there's nothing, Aegis even said it was okay."

"That's gotta be the work of Beldam… there's no graveyard out here, Av'ry. And no offense to your cat, but I don't trust 'im the slightest," he called back

"*As you shouldn't,*" Aegis purred.

The only fear she felt was rooted in the fact that somehow she had been able to see this graveyard clearly in her drugged state of sleep. Why was that? So far Moz had detected every danger so far along the path and he stood almost idle, no sense of alarm whatsoever.

"You stay here then," he called back to Tristan teasingly. "In the rare chance you're right and things go south."

Tristan grimaced and Avery turned back towards the iron gates. Moz was already lifting his arm to open it when she slapped his arm away from it. He looked at her with bewilderment, probably ready to call her all kinds of profanities again.

"What are you…"

Avery swung her rucksack down to open it and rummage through its contents. She didn't bother explaining to him as she pushed away her jeans and notebook and the other assorted items to reach the bottom of the bag. Just as she had expected; she found a small inventory of coins in gold, silver, bronze, and copper. She had packed none of them; somehow an instinct that had been buried told her they would be there.

She grabbed three of the small copper coins in her hand and put the rucksack back on. Leaning down, she arranged them into a triangle at the base of the iron doors.

"An offering?" Moz asked from behind her. If she didn't know any better, she could have sworn she heard an impressed tone in his voice.

She nodded, straightening up and stepping back a few paces away from the fence. Avery cleared her throat and puffed out her chest as bravely as she could muster before asking "May we enter?"

"*Clever girl*," Aegis remarked.

Moz looked at her with confusion and then back at the gate. Nothing happened. Avery realized very quickly it may have been a little bit ridiculous for the titanic bird to appear out of nowhere and caw with approval. She remained firm as long as she could, perhaps whoever would have let them in wanted to be certain her formality was sincere.

Minutes passed in silence, aside from Tristan's pleading for them to simply ignore the cemetery and press on. Naturally, Avery ignored him. Her confident pose shrunk inwards as she began to realize that this was nothing but a wild coincidence. Avery looked down at Aegis to see his demeanor had not changed at all. His tail remained swishing, looking at the gate as though he knew someone was about to let him inside. If he was so sure, she decided to wait a little longer.

There was a small caw above them and Avery threw her gaze upwards with bright excitement. A small crow flew above the clearing over their heads, over the cemetery and into the forest. It vanished as quickly as it had appeared. That had to be the sign!

Without waiting for Moz's reaction, Avery pushed open the cemetery gates. When she stepped inside she had expected the environment around her to grow darker as it had in the dream, but Tristan and the clearing were still where she had left them when she glanced over her shoulder.

The inside of the cemetery was not nearly as frightening as she had anticipated. Alongside the single footpath they walked on were small tomb markers, some were simple slabs of stone while others were intricately carved angels. Fresh flowers adorned many of them and left a sweet scent of larkspur and peony. Who would walk this deep into the haunted forest just to leave flowers at a tomb?

Her fear began to wane and she took careful steps further towards the center of the cemetery. Moz followed several paces behind her with silence, but her awareness of his presence in the rear-left of her skull followed her to the epicenter until he stopped. She turned around to see what had caused this sudden pause.

"Moz?" she asked when he didn't say anything, silently looking around the gravestones. He still had not drawn his sword, undoubtedly a good sign for her.

"I think I know where we are." He turned forward, not looking at her but past her left shoulder at the giant stone chair she stood before. "Balthazar."

She looked at him with her forehead scrunched in confusion, trying to make sense of the muddled name he had uttered. The soothing scent of the flora around them was replaced with a clove-laced tobacco smoke.

"*I have been waiting for you,*" a low, velvety voice called from over her left shoulder and she shrieked in surprise. She whirled around, back-pedaling towards Moz with her small dagger drawn towards the source of the voice.

The man towered far above Moz and Avery's heads even as he still rose from the earth. His legs stretched for miles in tailored pants the same shade as the darkened forest, the tails of his black suit jacket hitting the back of his knees. He brushed invisible dirt off his pristine, white shirt with a hand adorned in large, gold rings. Avery's attention was caught by a gold-plated ring of a corvid skull. She flicked her gaze up to his face, daring herself to not be afraid.

Though he was dressed to the nines, he smiled at them with black teeth dirtied from his trip to the surface.

A stripe of black face paint was glazed over the optical region of his face, covering his eyebrows and the bridge of his nose, and was only visible against his skin by the beading of sweat contrasting them. Locks of hair were pulled back into a leather tie underneath a gentleman's top hat, iridescent feathers and the same corvid skull adorning the front of it. He climbed into the giant chair, which was no more than a giant white stone block with a space to sit carved out. His movements were as fluid as water, the length of his legs crossing the space in a single bound.

He motioned towards Avery with a wave of his hand. "There's no need for that toothpick, we are friends here."

Avery looked down at her dagger, once again angry with how small her only defense was. Turning around, she saw Moz had still not even drawn his own weapon. Though his expression was still hard, it seemed more at ease than she had expected. Avery put away her dagger, looking toward the strange man.

"What are you doing here, Balthazar?" Moz asked.

"Helping a daughter, can't a man do that?" He looked at Avery's alarm-widened eyes and threw back his head in hearty laughter. "Not by blood, you're pale as paper!"

Avery frowned, taking another step away from the man and found herself next to Moz.

"I… I don't know what you mean."

The crow that had been circling above the graveyard plunged down from the sky, feet landing on Balthazar's right shoulder. He stood up, stretching taller and taller until he stood before them. Underneath the tobacco smoke Avery detected a scent of rot and she willed herself to not audibly gag. He looked at her with an amused gaze, one that was reflected in the beady eyes of the creature clinging to his shoulder bone.

"We used to be good friends, Avery Porter. And it seems we still have a lot to offer each other."

He looked at her as though waiting for a response but every bone in her body shook with fear and she could not will her tongue form any coherent words.

"She doesn't know shit right now," Moz finally offered. "And frankly I have no idea who she was so I can't help you there."

"This is Balthazar, the demon of the crossroads," Moz then said to Avery. "He stands between the living and the dead and as both the metaphorical and quite literal gatekeeper."

She glanced at Moz, both looking for some indication of truth to this statement and out of discomfort of Balthazar staring at her. So this demon dealt with the dead? That must mean that she had met him in her previous life when she died.

Looking back at the frightening figure she asked "Are all of the crossing souls your friends?"

Balthazar laughed once more, startling the crow and sending it in a frenzied launch back into the sky. "Ha, no! You were a special case! But don't let it get to your head, little bird. My wife and I have many daughters."

Obviously this demon was more than certain of who she had been before. "Why don't you just tell me? Since you clearly know who I was."

He stopped laughing and his expression went grim. "I don't work alone, you know. I can only tell you so much without receiving punishment from my mistresses. While I can't offer up what it is you seek most, I do have something that can help you get there."

Balthazar held his palms together at chest height and motioned them as though he were parting a pair of curtains. Avery gasped when a black hole opened in the ground between them, a small opening into an abyss.

"Reach in," Balthazar gently instructed.

She shook her head violently. "No way! If you think for even a second I'm going to-"

"Don't be a brat," Moz grumbled in annoyance, knocking her in the back of the knee with his to push her forward. "If he's offering help, don't be stupid about it."

"Thank you, Mr. Mosley," Balthazar said, accepting Moz's help to push Avery into reaching in.

Avery shot Moz a sour look before peering down at the hole. How was it possible for the earth to suddenly gape into nothing? How was any of this even possible? She got down onto her knees and looked inside, trying to see even an outline of anything the darkness contained. Then she looked up at Balthazar standing above her.

"Am I at the crossroads? Is that what's happening?"

He shook his head. "You're not dying, daughter. I come to you with sincere assistance. Now reach your hand in and grab it, but be careful."

Her curiosity got the best of her and she reached her hand into the pit. At first she expected her hand to fall off at the wrist or burn with an unseen fire, but it vanished behind the veil of the hole. She wiggled her fingers to assure herself of their continued attachment and found herself satisfied. It was as though she was reaching into an old room, the air around her hand feeling stale and colder than the late summer heat around the graveyard. Avery reached in further until she was elbow-deep in the nothingness. Her hands blindly slapped around the space and she yelped in surprise when it hit a velveteen wall.

Using the newly found surface, her hand travelled downwards until it found a surface perpendicular to the wall. Her fingers inched carefully forward until her shoulder was nearly submerged. As she blindly moved, her index finger was sliced on the pad and she winced at the unexpected pain.

"Something cut me," she hissed at the men angrily, knowing she had been deceived.

"Follow the blade until you find the hilt," was all Balthazar said.

She hadn't looked up at his face but knew he was finding joy in this game. Avery did as he instructed and let her finger follow the sharp metal edge, moving more carefully. Her finger grew warm with blood and she finally closed her hand around what must have been the cross guard of a sword. Maneuvering around it, she found the grip and hastily pulled it out of the black hole.

The blade was much longer and wider than she had expected, the space her hand had disappeared into must have been much larger than she thought. Its hilt was made of a lovat colored steel, the grip covered with a dark brown leather and necklace was draped carefully around it. On the brass chain was a glass circle, the matching case around it adorned at the top with metal roses and a small crow skull. In the middle of the sword's thick cross guard was a strange and leathery lump.

"What is that?" She asked.

Her knowledge of swords was quite limited but she had never seen such a thing on a hilt. Avery turned to Moz, certain that his assumed knowledge of swords would help. Instead his eyes were widened with recognition, staring at the sword.

"Hemlock."

Baffled, she began to ask him to repeat himself but then looked back at the sword. The leathery lump had opened to reveal a single eye. It was teeming with life, the golden iris flickering back and forth as though the sword was alive and observing its surroundings. She shrieked, dropping the sword on the ground. Both Moz and Balthazar flinched, and the demon picked it off the ground. He dusted dirt off the eyelids and blade before pulling the necklace off. Holding it in his palm, he extended it towards her.

"Have a little more respect, little bird. You're going to want to put this on," he advised. "You'll need it until you get your mojo back."

"My what?"

She hesitated for a moment before reaching out and taking the jewelry, shivering at how cold Balthazar's hand was. Avery unclasped the necklace and put it on, examining the glass ornament to figure out why she could have possibly needed it. As she did, Balthazar forced the grip of the sword back in her hand and she looked at him with surprise.

"Why do I need this?"

"Hold it up to your eye… look through it."

Avery didn't protest that time but immediately held the small lens up to her right eye, her left closed. She saw the graveyard around her tinted slightly cerulean from the glass. Misty white figures were added to the scene, much like those from her dream. Some were only mere shapes assumed to be humanoid, and others were formed into distinguished people with eyes and noses.

"They might not look like much now," Balthazar croaked. "But you'll soon become tuned so finely to see them, they will almost be alive again. Soon you won't even need the seeing glass."

Avery dropped the glass and it hit her sternum. Balthazar stooped down to reach into the black hole and pulled out a sheath. He stepped forward after the hole disappeared and held the sheath by the leather strap towards her. Avery reluctantly took it, sheathing the sword and using the strap to wear it on her shoulder.

Before she could speak, Moz took Balthazar by the arm and pulled him away. She couldn't hear what they were talking about when they were well away from her. They spoke almost toe-to-toe, Moz looked angry and Balthazar remained eerily jovial. Aegis slinked around her ankles; she had nearly forgotten he was there.

"What do you think they're talking about?"

"*And how should I know? It seems like Jack knows how to keep quiet. I don't trust either of them now*," he purred.

Moz shifted and his back was to them now. His voice escalated but she still couldn't make out any words. She began to inch forward with hopes of getting a better listen, but before she could get much closer Balthazar peered at her past Moz's right shoulder. Moz looked over his shoulder towards Avery and her eyes widened with alarm. Dark blood oozed out of his nostrils and threatened to spill over his top lip.

"Moz! Are you okay?"

Balthazar was the first to return. "Before I let you continue your journey, I insist that a companion join you. I feel he may be able to help you get your bearings back, Avery Porter. If I may, will you look through the seeing glass?"

She took the glass between her index finger and thumb, lifting it to her eye to peer through. Again she saw the misty forms, but beside Balthazar stood a new figure. He appeared to be maybe a year or two younger than her, with light hair hitting the middle of his ears. His small jaw was hardened in an empty expression, thick eyebrows hung over his golden eyes. He was dressed in a grey tunic and brown riding pants, unlike any attire Avery had ever seen in Ardua.

"This is Owen," Balthazar stated. "He died twenty six years ago from a fever in the countryside. Reaped by a girl who goes by the name Kit. Nice gal, by the way. He will help you along the way, or until you've come to your senses."

The young man opened his mouth as though he were speaking, but no sound came out. She dropped her glass and looked at Balthazar. "I can't hear what he's saying."

"You can't now, but you will. That's just part of the process," he told her. "Now I recommend getting back to your path, your companion grows impatient and worried."

She had almost forgotten about Tristan outside of the iron fence and the shouts of their names that had faded into the background. Catching a glimpse at Moz's face before walking ahead of her, she saw the blood was now smeared down his chin and still pouring. As they approached the entrance she became aware of the presence tagging along behind them, assumedly Owen.

When they reached Tristan he had been pacing back and forth at the foot of the fence. He looked up at them, first at Moz's gushing nose and then at the sword on Avery's back.

"Ave… tell me y' didn't," he groaned. She shook her head in confusion, not knowing what he had meant but still had a feeling the answer was no.

"It was a gift."

Moz attempted to wipe blood off his face with the back of his hand but only smeared it further. "Even better, she got us a tag-along. Some kid."

Tristan gave him a knowing look and shook his head once with slow action. "I felt a difference in the air. If he turns into a problem, he's outta here… you an' me though," he pointed at Moz. "We're talking later. For now, we have to keep going."

He was the first to trudge forward and Moz wiped the blood off his face, the flowing stopped now, before following him. Avery looked over her shoulder at the space the graveyard had occupied, now empty except for the small wildflowers that dotted the clearing.

"Uh, come on Owen," she wasn't sure how to address the spirit that hovered with them but knew she had to establish her leadership in this unlikely pairing. Though she couldn't see the spirit, a chill came over her in a small breath of air. Her shoulder buzzed with static as though the muscle had suddenly failed before becoming clear again. Avery stumbled in surprise before chasing after the men. Being alone with a ghost was not exactly something she felt comfortable with.

"*I still can't shake the feeling we're being watched,*" Aegis purred.

Avery whirled in every direction in an effort to search for any eyes that may have observed the encounter. The cemetery had vanished from where it had loomed only a moment ago, leaving nothing in the tall grass to indicate it had even been there. Her skin itched with the sensation of stares, but where?

"Hurry along, Ave," Tristan called out from several yards away when she realized she had come to a halt to scan the trees.

Her gaze slid to Moz. He was looking around casually but his expression remained indifferent when he met her look. If he still wasn't acting on vigilance, then she probably had nothing to worry about; he was always the first to draw. She looked down at Aegis near her feet as he watched the men, acting as though his observation was never made.

"Sorry, distracted now I guess," she apologized and hurried to follow.

"Are you sure she is cut out for the job?"

The soft whisper of concern from his wife hung in the air before falling to the forest floor. His corvid companion perched on his shoulder shifted its beady gaze to Balthazar, eagerly awaiting his response.

"She never failed you, my Queen. If you have even a faint glimmer of belief that she deserves a second chance, then I think we should let her have it," his voice seemed to be only a harsh croak cutting through the sweetness that Mona's words had left behind.

Mona looked over her shoulder at him, her hand still resting on the tree from where they had watched the group of Reapers. Skepticism hung heavy in her dark eyes but the eye contact he received from the goddess was blissful. Her full lips turned into a frown.

"My concern is with her guide."

"Aegis may be a stickler, but my brother knows that what the Beldam is doing is wrong. The only problem lies with making her familiar with the Necropolis, I do not believe he'd let that go over easily. Neither will William, I assume. They don't know why I am invested in the fall of the Knights."

Balthazar stooped low until his eyes were level with Mona's womb. Was she trembling? He raised his face to look up at hers. Her thick brows were raised in fearful skepticism.

"Do not fear," he put his hand over where the child was growing inside her as though it was all he needed to do to protect them from the Queen of Od. "The witches will end the Knights and we will get Ara's cleansing. I can lead them right to where your spell book is being kept, they can get much further than I could. This child will have no demonic nature, I swear it."

CHAPTER FIVE
THE EMPEROR

I say we eat them".

Moz flinched at the voice, startled by the clarity. He glanced at Tristan to his left without turning his head with the hope he didn't notice the small flicker of movement. No sign of alarm from the exorcist. He rubbed his hands on his pants for what could have been the millionth time that day, yet the blood still sat in the shallow crevices of his palms. Dried blood still remained flaked around the septum of his nose and philtrum. How he wished he could just wash himself of it.

His head pounded as the beast that had just spoken was slamming fists along the inside of his skull, demanding to be let out. It was not Jack who had just spoken, but something with intentions far graver than serving as a demonic companion. It rumbled low as thunder and crashed in his eardrums as tumultuous waves; part of him had nearly expected Tristan or Avery to hear it as well.

Tristan had given him a knowing glance after they had returned from Balthazar's graveyard after seeing Moz's blood pouring from his nostrils. Tristan knew what was happening and who was worming their way out of Moz, but he doubted Tristan anticipated it to actually happen.

He was the one who had found Moz in the field that day, blood pouring from his head the same way. Moz had been reduced to a seizing fit, screaming in tongues and nearly clawed out the eyes of the young man named Tristan Díomasaigh. Though the exorcism he performed on Moz had not been enough to fully rid him of the demon, it was kept at bay for the short lifetime of Tristan's daughter.

"It won't be much longer now," Balthazar had whispered to Moz in the cemetery. "You need to prepare them for the Knight because when it comes, there will be no mercy. Tell them how to hide, tell them how to run away."

He glanced over his shoulder to look at Avery following them. She followed behind from a reasonable distance, the seeing glass held up to her left eye and whirling around to see the forest around them through the eyes of the dead. There was no way on earth she would be able to outrun or conceal herself from a Knight of Od. What had the Priestess been thinking when she sent them to fetch her?

"I bet you could fit one hand around her entire neck... snap it until her eyes roll back in her head," the demon spoke again.

Moz felt as though he were lifting his hands to grasp it and throw it against the inside wall of his head. It laughed and slinked away back into the dark mist lingering on the outer edge of his mind where he did not dare to venture.

He looked ahead of him once more, this time Tristan was facing him and making a point of his skeptical expression. Moz scowled and walked faster so that he would not have to participate in the lecture that surely would have ensued. Jack had been riding on his shoulder since leaving the cemetery but the rat placed a small paw on Moz's neck and sat upright to see what was wrong.

"*Master, are you back?*"

He peered at the small animal, putting a smile on his face to the best of his ability. When the Knight lingering inside made itself vocal or tried engaging Moz, Jack was kicked off the channel. There was enough room for only one demon in his skull at a time.

"I think this is a good time to stop for a brief period of time," Moz decided, the guilt perfectly hidden in his lukewarm tone. Tristan looked at him with confusion, scratching his head.

"We haven't left the cemetery even an hour ago, what are you—"

"Look, Avery has a weapon now. A pretty good one, too. If you don't want her swinging it around wildly, I think taking ten minutes to show her something will benefit us more."

Moz ignored the scowl on Avery's face.

"Draw your weapon," he ordered as he took his own sword out of its sheath. Avery hesitated at first, but drew Hemlock from her back sheath without further questions.

"I want you to take swings at me, do your best to make a hit," he held his sword upwards and kept his relaxed stance. She held the sword with both hands, clearly uncomfortable with the heavy weight of it as she wobbled on the balls of her feet.

"But I don't want to hurt you."

"If I thought you could land a hit on me, we wouldn't be doing this."

She scowled with anger, her dark eyebrows furrowing down. Avery held up her sword and charged at him, her speed much slower than he was used to from an opponent, yet she was quicker than he had anticipated from her on the first try. He stood relaxed as she swung horizontally and with a flick of his sword, they clashed in contact.

Avery scowled as they stood blade-to-blade, trying to overpower him with sheer force. Moz let her push as hard as she wanted, looking down at her freckled nose before carefully shoving her back.

"You used your arms. That would work if you had a one-handed sword, but this one will require all of your strength behind each swing. Use your hips, put some power behind it."

Avery swung her arm again, this time shifting her weight on her hips in a rotation to push the blow harder. It struck Moz's weapon with a louder clang than it did before and he shoved back, knowing this was a real spar.

Whatever life she had been living before they retrieved her must have provided some sort of athleticism; she was keeping up with his steps. She jumped onto a fallen tree, her feet finding its surface with ease and carrying her just out of reach of his blade. Avery leaped at him, swinging her sword downwards to bring it upon him, though he knew that she was quite terrified of actually making contact. Moz made no attempt to be slow as he dodged and her face warped with surprise when he was suddenly yards away and she fell into open air. He charged at her, his dominant shoulder reeling back to swing.

The sword was knocked from his hand and clattered against the tree feet away from him before falling to the ground. Moz skid to a stop to avoid crashing into Avery's sword and he looked at his sword on the ground in bewilderment.

"Moz... I can see him now," Avery whispered.

The revenant stood between them, heaving from over-exertion. His features were more saturated with color than they had been in the graveyard. Avery looked at Moz's sword that had been thrown out of his grip out of nowhere, then at Owen.

Owen bent forward with his hands on his knees to gather up strength before speaking. He straightened out and his face warped with anger, his mouth opening wide and moving fast as though he was trying to yell. Avery still heard no words, but rather a muffled drone. Past his shoulder she saw Moz's confused expression passing right through the ghost towards her.

"Owen… he disarmed you…" she blurted. "Knocked the sword right out of your hand… how can a spirit do that?"

Owen turned his attention from Moz to her and out of fright she dropped her own weapon. The muffled yelling was louder as he faced her but she could still not discern any words. Past the two of them, she saw Tristan drawing out several of his vials.

"He's become violent, I reckon we've no use for the ghost," he boomed and leapt off the stone he had been perched on.

"No!" Avery reacted louder than she meant to, holding her hands defensively in front of her as though she were the one about to be exterminated. "I mean, don't yet. I don't think he's violent, I think he's just supposed to be protective… I think that's what Balthazar wanted him to do."

Moz walked to pick up his sword, wiping it with the end of his dark green shirt before sheathing it. "She's right. Balthazar explicitly said he was supposed to help."

Tristan grimaced before putting away his clinking, violet vials. He folded his arms and looked at them with obvious agitation. Avery laid Hemlock carefully on the ground as she looked at Owen's back and was able to see Tristan on the other side through the gentle transparency. She approached the spirit, her empty hands held up in front of her to show him that everything was okay enough to leave her weapon on the ground. As she grew closer, the hairs on her arms stood up atop gooseflesh and a cold static expanded all the way to her shoulders.

"Owen," she managed to say after swallowing twice in order to get herself to speak. "They're not going to hurt either of us and I know you're not going to hurt them, right?"

He turned towards her and she quickly pulled back her hands, one of them fumbling for the seeing glass to hold it up to her eye. Through the tinted glass his colors were much more vivid, but he still seemed to be made of wisps of smoke. Balthazar made it seem that Owen would slowly fade into existence to her. The anger built into the darkness of his eyebrows slowly faded in the silence held by the three of them and he made no effort to speak.

"I need you to let us do this," she continued. "So I can defend myself, so I won't die."

His eyes widened momentarily and the youth that had been apparent before his rage returned; the poor boy couldn't have been a day over sixteen when he died. His expression softened as he nodded - the first intelligent response she had received from him. Her heart pounded at the realization of what she was doing: not only was Avery speaking to the dead, the dead were answering.

Owen stepped aside out of her reach with the tiniest hint of a smile on his face as though to grant her permission. Avery dropped the seeing glass and looked at him, once again he was made more of light than he was of flesh. She picked up her sword and turned back around to Moz.

"This time, don't go easy on me!"

"Just get on already!"

The shout of a man came from behind Lily as she slowly scaled the gangplank, her hands balled into fists at her sides as she tried not to look down at the wide gap between the pier and the side of the tri-masted ship. She inhaled deeply before scurrying up the rest of the plank, fearing for her life by the time she threw herself onto the deck.

Lily heard grumbling from over the side of the deck as Morgana turned around, her eerie smile directed back at her. The spidery woman brushed dirt off her riding pants and folded her arms. Though she did not seem as rigid as she had been within the police headquarters, Lily still felt uneasy with the way Morgana spoke to her and looked at her. She had given Lily clothes the night before as they were preparing the ship, similar black riding pants that sat with unfamiliarity on the curves of her hips. The loose blouse she now wore was the color of cream and contrasted against her umber arms with the long sleeves rolled up.

She approached Morgana, who was busying herself with a map she had laid out on a crate. Lily put her hands on her hips, making no attempt to hide her frustration when the woman finally looked up at her.

"When are you going to clue me in on what's going on?"

Morgana smiled with the bone-chilling grin. "The world out there is a savage place, far lacking in technology and advancement. No cars, no phones, no media of any kind. They call Ardua the City of the Blessed. We may as well be our own universe!"

The woman paced to a chest at the base of the center mast. Opening it, she pulled out a bow of walnut wood with a quiver of brown leather. The arrows it contained were adorned with feathers of every variety. Morgana held them out towards her.

"I understand you partake in archery as a hobby?"

"I- I mean," Lily stammered "yeah, at the university, but I never-"

"Do not worry, my dear! We have found two of our best men to accompany you! You will never be placed in severe danger!"

Specifically *severe* danger? Just when Lily thought the woman could not become any creepier, the smile that stretched over her gaunt face made Lily consider running back down the gangplank and all the way home. She knew if she did that there would be no one there to welcome her. She swallowed hard and clenched her fists, turning them inwards at her sides.

"Excellent," was all she could say.

Lily snatched the bow and quiver out of Morgana's hands, slipping underneath the braided leather strap to wear the quiver on her back. The woman smiled down at her before turning to return to her leadership duties.

It had not been quite an hour before the ship parted with the dock and Lily observed their departure from the stern of the ship. The port of Ardua grew smaller and smaller as they traveled further into the Stillmaw Sea, the lanterns lighting up one by one until they became distant stars in the falling dusk.

"Miss?" a man's voice asked from behind her.

Lily turned around to face a man only slightly taller than her. His ginger hair was shaved close to his scalp in a short fuzz, thickly framed glasses sat perched on his bony nose. He was dressed in a similar fashion, though his shirt not nearly as loose as hers and was covered by a sort of leather armor pad over his chest.

"I'm Peter," he introduced himself in a calm voice. "I was one of the officers who followed the murderers into the woods, I saw your friend alive and well."

Lily nearly buckled at the knees in relief and she clutched herself at the heart. "Thank Ara!"

He nodded in agreement with her cry. "I'll be one of the officers to accompany you to finding them. This is my partner, Iggy," he gestured to the taller man who stood behind him.

Iggy towered over Lily and she had to look upwards to properly greet him. His dark hair was shaved down as well, his dark eyebrows flat with stoicism. She looked skeptically at Iggy and then back to Peter.

"Doesn't talk much, that one," Peter explained and scratched the back of his head. She had expected the taller man to hold that air of sternness but instead he smiled, clearly able to handle the teasing from his partner.

"Thank you both so much," she thanked them in a whisper. "I can't even begin to tell you how much it means to me that you're doing this, helping me find Avery."

"Don't worry at all. We'll find her."

When the two men returned to their duties, the fire of Morgana's hair caught the corner of her eye. She was bent slightly toward the starboard side of the ship where it met the stern, a bird perched along the rail next to her. Her lips were moving as though she was talking to the magnificently colored peregrine, the bird moving its head in a twitching manner in a response to her words. While she couldn't make out the words, Morgana sounded angry. The bird flapped its wings thrice before launching itself into the sky, back west towards the coast they had just left.

Lily watched the woman straighten her spine and dust herself off as if the creature had left some sort of grime on her. When she caught Lily staring, a smile spread across her face.

Lily backpedaled, clutching her new bow against her. If she stayed around this woman any longer the image of her fluorescent teeth would be burned into her brain forever. She turned on her heel to walk down the steps. To her surprise, she did not hear Morgana call out from behind her nor any protest to her departure. She spun in a circle when she reached the main deck, unsure of where she was to go.

In the mere periphery of her eye a streak of dark mossy green slinked across the wooden deck. Lily turned her stare to the snake as it oscillated forward and she shrieked. The officers around her flinched with reaction, some drawing their swords as though to react to the threat. Seconds later, they connected the sudden scream to the snake wriggling in the dim light and they returned to their duties. She felt her face flush with anger, how could they be okay letting a serpent roam the deck? Lily searched the forces to find someone who looked friendly enough to ask for help.

It wasn't until then that she noticed the animals that had blended in so perfectly to their chaotic surroundings. A luminous fox had taken a seat next to a man opening box crates, not watching him but seeming to oversee everything else happening on the ship with sharp eyes. The iridescent form of a crow sat perched on the shoulder of a woman passing by and into the lower decks. Birds, hounds, foxes, predatory cats, and what sounded like a bear coming from the decks below. How could she have missed all of them when she boarded the ship? The beasts were clearly wild creatures, yet there was organization and an overall calmness on board that gave them the illusion of domestication.

Lily turned to find a safe place to hide, but not before catching a look from Morgana. For that brief moment, an aura of darkness surrounded her. Her ginger brows dug down deep into the top of her nose and her mouth clenched so sternly that it seemed she would let out a roll of thunder if she spoke. Then the eerie smile came upon Morgana's face as she locked eyes with Lily before the woman disappeared into the crew.

— ❦ —

By the time night fell, Avery's knees threatened to buckle under her weight with every step she took. Walking for hours during the previous day had been difficult, but she now had to do it with the massive sword strapped to her back. Even Aegis proved his fatigue hours before and had asked to be placed in her rucksack again rather than be forced to walk any further. She wished it was as easy for her to simply lay down on a pile of clothes and rest.

"We should make our food and camp here before it gets too late," Moz suggested, throwing down his rucksack.

Moz didn't appear to be affected at all by exhaustion, his quick pace was maintained and there were several instances when both he and Tristan had to wait for Avery to catch up. They used a lot of that time to catch small animals, a slain rabbit and squirrel hung from a rope in Tristan's hand. Avery squirmed at the thought of eating them, but she was wise enough to know that she didn't have any other option. The vegetation in that cursed forest was nothing she desired to eat as she had no scientific knowledge of what plants were poisonous or not. So she trusted the men; though she didn't have to like their methods of satiety.

Avery set down her pack, opening the top to let Aegis out. She had expected a snarky response from the demon companion, but she was met with silence as the cat continued to sleep on top of her folded leather jacket. After stripping herself of the sheathed sword, she crumpled to the ground next to the pack in exhaustion. From where she laid on her back she peeked between her bent knees to see Tristan breaking off low-hanging branches and throwing them into the patch of bare dirt that Moz was clearing.

It wasn't long before a cone of branches sat in the dirt, Tristan saving a long one in his hand. Moz rummaged through his pack and pulled out his black matchbook and one of his rolled tobacco cigarettes. After lighting the roll held between his teeth, he stood up and dropped the still-lit match into the cluster of branches and leaves. The fire started out in twinkling embers before catching on the dried leaves, growing into a crackling heat.

Owen's ghostly figure stepped past her but he made no sound on the forest floor as he approached the fire with hands held forward. She heard underwater mumbling as he spoke, louder than it was hours before but she was still not able to decipher any of the words. He looked over his shoulder at her, the frustration on his face very clear.

Past him, Tristan impaled the bodies of the small animals on the stick he held before rotating it over the fire to act as a spit. Avery winced at the sight upon sitting upright and tucked her face into her bent knees. She felt a movement of air next to her and she turned her head sideways to see Owen sitting next to her now, his legs crossed and knees flesh against the ground like a waiting child. She sighed in exasperation when he spoke without sound and her frustration only grew. Ignoring the mumbling, she looked at Tristan.

"How much longer do you think we'll be out here?"

"With this pace? Three or four days I reckon," he answered as he turned the spit stick, sitting as far away from the sparking heat of the fire as he possibly could.

"Wow," her voice was quiet with discouragement. "I didn't realize the forest was that vast… we're not even halfway."

She saw Tristan shrug. "It's best to take it easy, there's no tellin' what we'll see on the way and I reckon we make sure we keep as high a stamina as possible rather than travelin' fast."

"And you know who's going to be waiting for us on the other side," Moz chimed in.

Avery had been mindlessly stripping a small twig of its leaves and tossed it into the fire as she listened. "I thought Morgana and her officers wouldn't come into the forest?"

"And they won't. But I'll bet you anything they're travelling around the coastline to intercept us on the west edge of the forest."

"Aye, if the lot of 'em got to Centralia before us that would be rotten luck," Tristan added. "That's where the rest of us are and I doubt they'd be expectin' it."

"While they do have currents and doldrums working against them, they also have the advantage of moving constantly while we have to rest. It's hard to say," Moz said. The group fell into silence after the uncertainty was noted.

Even after making it out of the forest alive, an enemy Avery had not even come face to face with yet would be waiting for them. She barely figured out how to swing her sword the right way and she was supposed to battle? She hoped "the rest of us" were far more prepared than she was.

Images of the slain officer at the river vibrated in her head, the sound of the splashing in the water. Why had Moz let the other two go? After seeing him slay both the officer and the possessed man, she didn't doubt his capability to attack the remaining officers.

Send me everything you have next time, I'll kill them all.

She hoped for their sake that Moz could back up his arrogance with skill. The two officers could have been handled right then and there, but the way Tristan had spoken about Morgana's legion made it seem they were the ones in a minority. How many Reapers were backing the plans of the Knights?

Avery poked at the muscle above her left knee, aching from the travel over the rough terrain. Remembering what Tristan taught her the previous day, she sat up. She pulled the retired dagger out of the front pocket of her rucksack and cut a vertical slit three inches long in the front of her shirt at the hem. Taking the exposed threads between her fingers, she ripped hard all the way around the bottom of her shirt until the other side was cut loose and she held a long strip of fabric in her hand. Using her palm to hold one end flesh against her sore muscle, she wrapped the fabric around her knee for support and tied off the end. Though her shorter shirt now revealed part of her belly and the bandaged wound, she wasn't alarmed by the exposure. Despite the anger these two near-strangers invoked in her, Avery knew they weren't creeps.

The smell of burning meat singed her nose and Avery grimaced when Tristan took the cooked animals off of the spit. He began slicing off pieces and handed a bit of rabbit to Moz before offering some to her. She hesitated at first but accepted the rabbit reluctantly.

"For all you know, he could have poisoned that," a voice unexpectedly whispered next to her right ear. Avery shrieked, dropping the burnt meat in the dirt and launching upwards off the ground. She spiraled around and looked down at Owen, still sitting with crossed legs.

"W-was that you?!"

"What's wrong with you," she heard Moz snap from behind her, but her eyes were still locked with bewilderment on Owen. His face darkened but kept his gaze set on Avery. He stood up, face-to-face with her.

"Are you going to keep letting him get away with speaking to you like that?"

She had not been mistaken, Owen's voice was crystal clear now as though he had surfaced from underneath a muffled surface. Her eyes were wide and she stammered trying to find a reply.

"I... I can hear him now," was all she could say, directed at the two men rather than towards the specter. Owen's fierce expression changed to sudden shock.

"You can hear me now! This will make things much easier," the revenant cried out happily.

"What's he sayin," Tristan asked. She watched Owen's expression quickly soften and he slowly shook his head side to side. Did he not want her to relay any information or suspicion he had?

"He was in the middle of a thought. It didn't make any sense."

He gave her a nod of gratitude, the soft gaze he held never broke. Avery subtly turned her head to look at him and he seemed as physical and real as Moz and Tristan. Light reflected over his cheekbones the way it did over hers and he disrupted the surface of the dirt where he sat.

"Thanks for that," he whispered softly as though he might be heard by anyone other than her. "I just have a bad feeling about them and I'm not entirely sure on it."

"That's a fair judgement," she chuckled and tried to keep her voice low as well. Despite the flames she had fixed her gaze upon, she felt the air next to her shoulder grow cold.

"It is not funny. Anyone who knows Balthazar on such a personal basis usually has horrible reasons."

She turned the thought over several times in her head as she watched them. Tristan had regarded the cemetery with unhindered superstition and fear; Moz walked to the demon of the crossroads and treated him as an old friend. Maybe it made sense; as a Reaper it would not have been too outlandish to come in contact with the crossroads and whoever stood there. She had never bothered to find out what happened after she gently touched her doomed souls. Did they go to Balthazar after her? Maybe Moz took the departed directly to him?

"Owen, we're Reapers. Like the one who took you away all those years ago. I don't think it's too bizarre for them to know each other," she offered with the intention of solidifying her wobbly theory by saying it out loud.

He glared at her with skepticism. "I'm not convinced just yet. But I do have some information you'll probably need. About that sword you got."

"Hemlock?"

Owen nodded, patient with the question she realized was redundant. "You probably already noticed from the eye, but Hemlock is a living thing. To make it do your bidding, you have to feed it."

"My bidding? What the fuck does that mean? I'm not exactly sure how to feed a sword, pardon my ignorance."

He shook his head. "Hemlock takes a minor blood sacrifice, real easy to just make a cut with the blade. Drips right down to its hilt. If you do this, spirits will manifest from wherever they are around you and fall under your control. They can actually create quite a bit of damage."

The ridiculous disbelief must have shown on her face when Owen looked at her and laughed. "Why would such a thing exist? I mean, where did it come from?"

"Hemlock came from the Necropolis," he said. "If you don't know that already, that's the Beldam's domain beneath Yve's. City in Od, actually. Occupied by mostly demons and foul souls. And Paion..."

"Beldam crafted Hemlock as a gift to the god of war in thanks for his assistance in creating the Knights, from what I've heard," he continued. "A demon named Rin stole it before Paion could receive it, but I'm not sure how it got into Balthazar's hands. Or why you have it now. I can only imagine what the world would be like if Rin hadn't done that. So stupid, but I'm thankful."

"Why would Paion help her?"

"Same reason anyone does anything: power."

Moz suddenly came to a halt, drawing his sword much sooner than Tristan and Avery did. She set Aegis on the ground to grip her weapon with both hands, holding it in front of her defensively. It was quickly becoming a second nature for her to draw her sword when Moz stopped unexpectedly.

"Something is up there, right?" she asked, meaning the top of the shallow ravine they had been traveling through. The forest itself answered her question with a snap of twigs cracking above them.

"Ground hasn't been misplaced, so whatever it is, it's small," Moz mumbled. He started forward slowly on the path that would lead them to the top, never turning his back towards the source of the sound. Before he could travel very far, the animal came into view.

The black wolf crept down from the top of the hill with careful movement visible in the pedaling of its haunches. Low growls were carried down towards them and became gradually louder as it maneuvered down to them. Yet Moz made no action.

"Run!" she yelled and began sprinting back in the direction from which they came. Tristan grabbed her by the rucksack before she could travel far and she fell off her feet with the yank, held up by his fist.

"It's a demon guide."

Moz sheathed his weapon. "Ina," he called out to the large wolf and crouched down to be face level when it approached him. The animal was clearly familiar with him, nuzzling the side of Moz's head and stretching back in a playful bow.

"This is Shank's guide," he explained. "You'll meet them when we get there."

The wolf took notice of Avery standing with her sword drawn at her side. Its lips snarled with a deep growl and leaned back in a low crouch to cross the five feet between them.

"I reckon you want to put the sword away when trying to meet Ina," Tristan advised, trying to soothe the wolf by gently scratching its back.

Avery was not sure what she should do to avoid being ripped to shreds by the sharp teeth on display. She slowly lowered her sword to the ground and laid it flat in the dirt, stepping slowly a foot forward as though to conceal it from the creature. She crouched low as she saw Moz do and raised a hand in front of her, limp in the air.

Ina shifted forward out of an attack-ready position and her icy eyes shifted to a more calm expression. Ina moved towards her slowly, nose against the ground and sniffed as she walked with caution. The wolf reached Avery's hand and she flinched at the damp feeling of Ina's nose against her sweaty skin. Ina's large frame overpowered Avery as she waited with held breath in a crouch.

After a long moment of sniffing, Ina leaned into Avery's neck and nearly knocked her off the balls of her feet to the ground. It seemed to be an affectionate gesture and Avery let out the breath she had been holding for dear life.

Avery regained her balance and pet the side of the animal's neck, confident that she had won her trust.

"I don't know who your Reaper is, but they sure are lucky to have someone so protective and sweet," she said to Ina.

Aegis stood at her feet and Ina took notice of him, sniffing the air around his head. She could sense the agitation from her cat, but Avery couldn't help but laugh.

"She said she tracked Moz through a piece of his clothing at home. Not bad for a dumb beast. Sent to guide us through the final leg of the forest."

"She tracked him this far by scent?"

"*No, by energy,*" he scoffed. "*To familiars, each person has a unique footprint. It radiates but I'm sure Ina can pick it up at a much greater distance than I am able to.*"

She tilted her head questioningly. "What does mine look like?"

Aegis laughed. "*If I had a way of describing it, believe me girl, I would. I suppose if I had to put a color to it, it would be green.*"

CHAPTER SIX
THE HIEROPHANT

As they broke through the last tree line and met with the rolling grassland, Ina cried out in a long howl. Avery's ears rang as it reverberated against the small hills and back towards them. The anticipation and excitement emanating from Moz and Tristan was tangible now as they neared the place they claimed was their home. Ina padded past them before breaking into a run, disappearing from the top of the first hill that sat outside of the tree line. Despite their happy air of eagerness, the men trudged as slowly as Avery did.

"Shouldn't we run to catch up?"

Tristan shrugged. "Nah, we know where we are. The shack's right up ahead."

She knew she should have been put off by his choice of words - "shack"- but the thought of simply throwing herself onto a floor and resting for hours was so appealing that she didn't care. She longed to wash the blood from her clothes and dress her wounds properly.

The final hills that lay before them somehow felt like the hardest part of the journey despite the destination right before them. Hemlock seemed heavier and heavier with every step she took as though it had been gaining mass for the past few days. Ina began howling from somewhere in front of them and she came into view as they topped the hill.

Before them, the last of the hills gradually became still into a flat grassland. A hundred yards in front of them, the lone wood structure sat waiting for them with a frown of sagging wood. From this distance it looked to have been haphazardly thrown together to vaguely resemble a house with a slanted roof, all from mismatching planks.

"Is that the place?"

"Aye, Moz and I built it ourselves! What do y'think?" the giant beamed down at her with a proud grin on his face. Though Owen snickered from beside her, she tried to do better at hiding her distaste. She shot the spirit a glare to silently scold him.

"It's definitely got character," she answered.

"Well, here she comes," Moz noted from behind them.

Avery hadn't noticed the two faint figures standing in front of the sagging structure until he pointed the one that ran in their direction. She saw the black buzzing clouds around where their heads should have been. Whoever they were, they were Reapers as well.

"She?"

Before he could muster up an answer, the figure was already near and practically upon them. As she ran, the black cloud fell away from her face until she came into clear view. She was a young woman around Avery's age, her complexion the color of terracotta. On her back was a quiver and her bow waved wildly in her hand as she ran, the black hair cut to her shoulders bouncing with every stride she took.

The woman spread her built arms wide and threw her bow to the ground, scooping the three of them into as tight an embrace as she could. Avery's eyes went wide with discomfort as she was pressed against Tristan's large side and between Moz and this total stranger.

With her face between Avery's shoulder and Tristan's bicep, she cried out. "We were so worried about you! We thought for sure you would be back before Kurosaki and Alice!"

She felt Moz wriggle away from the hug from behind her and Avery seized the opportunity to escape as well. His expression had suddenly grown dark.

"They're here?"

The woman's dark brown eyes were fixed on Moz, cat-like and thickly framed with lashes as her expression changed to a chastising glare.

"Don't forget that you need them when you're at each other's throats."

There was no reply from Moz but she didn't have to turn around to know his usual look of contempt. The young woman finally took notice of Avery's presence and was aware of this awkward meeting. She smiled, the smoothness of her nose scrunched up with a sincere expression of kindness.

"I hope they weren't too awful to you. I'm Maria."

Before Avery had a chance to return the greeting, Maria took notice of her blood-stained clothing. Her kind expression turned to a disgusted frown directed at Tristan and then to Moz.

"You just let her wander around in this? You probably had the entire forest on top of her, shame on you!" Maria grabbed Avery by the hand, turning around towards the direction she came from and began pulling her along. She looked over her shoulder at Moz and Tristan for any protest, but there was none.

"Let's find you some cleaner clothes, some that won't peg you as someone from the city. What's your name?"

Avery hadn't noticed until Maria mentioned the difference in their clothing. She was dressed similarly to Owen, though her red tunic was worn with rolled-up sleeves and fitted dark pants flaunted a curvier silhouette rather than sitting loosely around her legs. The men had mentioned she was in for a culture shock after leaving Ardua, but just how different was the city from everywhere else?

She turned around and saw Moz and Tristan behind them, trudging at a much slower pace than Maria's excited dragging. When she turned back she was met with Maria looking at her with enormous, waiting eyes.

"Oh, Avery."

"We're glad you're here, Avery," she said warmly. "I'm not even exaggerating! The High Priestess of Centralia told Moz to go find a Reaper within the city, and I can only assume she meant you! Look, Shank's waving!"

She pointed with her other hand at the lone figure still standing at the foot of the wood house before waving wildly back. Avery saw Ina's black form pacing around their feet as they waved.

"C'mon, let's go home," Maria chirped and hurried back towards the shack, scooping her bow back up into her hands.

As they grew closer and the black swarm faded, she saw that the figure waiting for them was a young man. His complexion was deep and he was quite tall, perhaps standing eye-to-eye with Moz. When he stopped waving, he bent forward to rustle Ina's fur playfully before standing back upright as they approached.

His hair was worn in long locks, thick and black. When he stood back up, the expression in his eyes greeted them with familiarity and friendliness despite Avery having never met him before.

"Their name is Shank," Maria announced, gesturing with flat hands towards Shank before sweeping them in Avery's direction. "And h...her?"

Maria trailed off, hesitant with her choice of pronouns until Avery nodded her head with attempted subtlety.

"Her name is Avery," Maria beamed.

Maria let go of Avery's hand and stepped back as though to encourage a conversation between the two of them. She felt her cheeks flush red as they stared at her.

"Hello there, Avery," Shank's voice was as warm and kind as she had expected it to be.

Avery took notice of Owen at her side, his face turning downwards in a scowl that nobody but her could see. She cleared her throat before attempting to hide her sheepishness, swinging her knapsack off her back to let Aegis out. He jumped hastily before she had even set the bag on the ground. Maria let out a sigh of adoration as Aegis circled around Ina's feet, the pair of familiars passing mere tolerance of each other.

"What a lovely cat! Is it your familiar, I'm assuming?"

Avery nodded. "Aegis can be a pain sometimes, but he's rather helpful. I'm glad he's here."

As she spoke, Maria had knelt down, her hand reaching to pet Aegis's side. He wriggled away in displeasure before sitting down yards away from her.

"He's very slow to warm up to people, so don't take that personally," she added.

"That's quite alright," Maria stood back up and brushed herself off. "You probably already know it, but Ina's the sweetest thing on four legs. Shank got pretty lucky with that one."

Avery bent down to stroke Ina's thick fur, carefully pulling out small twigs and leaves that had caught in the thick layer. She was right, the beautiful beast was still surprisingly docile and calm. Ina's lungs could be felt heaving with deep breaths of recovery, her giant body shrugging with each inhale.

"Where's your familiar?"

When Avery posed the question, Ina's ears went rigid and an air of silence fell over the group. Shank shifted their weight, made visibly uncomfortable by the question. The brief moment of quiet could already be noted as uncharacteristic of Maria as she had chattered happily the entire time since meeting. Her face was expressionless before she pulled the corners of her lips up into a forced smile.

"Well, you see… Croxi was an osprey. He was fine for years, a very trustworthy and kind demon companion. I don't know why it happened, but two years ago he just snapped. We had to put him down. Tristan did it."

Sadness washed over Maria's face as she gave up on the charade that the death of her familiar didn't hurt her. Avery felt a pang of guilt for asking even though she knew she had no way of knowing. Maria looked over her left shoulder towards the hills from where they had come from. Moz and Tristan were approaching; though they were out of earshot Maria still whispered.

"Did you notice it," she asked while rubbing her eyebrow with one finger.

Avery shook her head, not recognizing the gesture or what it was supposed to mean.

"Damn near pecked out Moz's eyeball," Shank chimed in. "Left that nice scar to show for it, too."

When the men finally joined their group Avery was crouched low on the ground and ignoring their jovial conversation. Instead she stared at Aegis, who was grooming himself in the dry grass.

What would cause a familiar to turn against their Reaper? Tristan had mentioned before to be wary of the demonic familiars, perhaps he had meant situations such as Moz being attacked by one. She had no doubt that Aegis was capable of attacking her if he desired to, with how sly and cunning he had proven to be.

"You're wary of him too now, aren't you?"

She tilted her head to the side thoughtfully after Owen spoke, answering only when she had reassured herself. "I don't think Aegis would kill me, he could have already if he truly wanted to. Though I'm not sure how he would do it."

Aegis dropped his paw and sat up to meet Avery's stare. *"Well, I suppose I could have clawed your skin to oblivion until you bled out. But I admit it's kind of nice having you around, girl."*

With a swishing tail he sat upright and followed the group as they disappeared through a red painted door into the shack.

"Aegis?" She could hear the bewilderment in Owen's voice. "I meant the gaunt one - Moz. What could he have done to make Croxi lash out?"

"I don't know. Why don't you eavesdrop on him and find out? He can't see or hear you."

Owen huffed. "As if I haven't tried that already! Whatever it is, he's keeping it tight under wraps."

When she looked over to glare at him he had already vanished, assumedly to the same place he goes whenever he is through talking. Perhaps it was to Balthazar's otherworldly cemetery. She stood up and sighed, her agitation with Owen was growing for how much he had insisted his paranoia of Moz was well justified.

She walked through the front door that had been left open just wide enough for Aegis to slink through. To her surprise, the interior seemed to belong to a cozy home rather than a worn down shack. Its contents mismatched and Avery guessed that each item was lifted from a different location, the bench with worn green cushions a far cry from the mining lanterns illuminating the room.

Avery had stepped into what must have been the kitchen, a wood burning stove cramped a little too closely against a basin to her right. Before her was a living room, or rather a mash of different mats and chairs. An abused wooden table sat low on top of a woven mat, haphazardly strewn papers and coffee stained metal cups sitting atop it.

Ina padded past the table and threw herself down on a stuffed cushion in the corner underneath the only window, one of its four panes made of blue salvaged glass. More cushions were strewn about to serve as seats in front of a large metal bowl littered with charcoal and ash, perhaps used in place of an indoor fireplace during the cold winters. Doorways lacking any kind of a door led off from the right wall into two rooms and Avery could see that one contained a thick bed mat on the floor and a series of boots lined next to it. Opposite that wall, an array of objects were hung on the left side of the main room: decorative arrows, hunting arrows, maps, drawings, dried flowers, a horseshoe.

The home didn't seem nearly large enough to house so many people but before Avery could ask how they all made it work, Maria swooped in and grabbed her by the hand. Avery's cheeks flushed red; a girl had never been so brazen with her.

"Let's get you cleaned up and into some new clothes!"

She was pulled back outside, much to her confusion. Maria led her around to the other side of the shack. Another wood structure sat yards away - a stable, from the faint neighing of horses. Maria was heading towards a pump ten feet away from the side of the house and Avery felt her eyes widen.

"We didn't have the resources to build a fancy well," Maria explained as though the pipe jutting out of the ground was the only thing that was surprising Avery. "There used to be structure here, but it was taken out by a fire. Luckily this pump remained!"

She hooked the metal handle of the bucket underneath the spout, turning the faucet on. Water sprayed them at first before becoming a steady stream. After the bucket was filled Maria put her hand on her hip and carried the bucket with the other in an awkward fashion into the shade of the roof eaves.

"This should be just enough to get the blood off. Later I'll show you the actual bath. Let me know when you're done and I'll give you fresh clothes," she chattered before disappearing back in the shack, leaving Avery by herself.

She peeled off her boots and socks, dumping out twigs and clumps of dirt. Before taking off her shirt to wipe off any remaining blood, she quickly looked around to make sure she was truly alone. No sign of anyone and no sign of Owen. She hurriedly used the cloth that had been tied to the handle of the bucket to wipe off dirt until she was satisfied before she returned indoors.

Maria had been waiting on the bench, one leg bouncing on top of her knee. She immediately shot up when Avery entered. Before Avery could say anything, Maria had already jumped over several cushions and grabbed her by the elbow.

"You're going to stick out like a sore thumb if you stay in those clothes! Come with me!"

Maria dragged her towards one of the open rooms and she was tripping over her own feet trying to keep up. How was it possible for someone to have that much energy? Avery huffed, but she complied. She seemed friendly enough.

In the room was a sleeping mat to the left of the door. On the opposite wall only a few yards away was a bureau, the wood chipped and a few corners were knocked off. Maria opened the doors with arms thrown outward in dramatic gusto to behold its contents. Clothing of every color was crammed into the tiny space, from deep crimsons to the softest of pinks.

"You are quite skinnier than me," she noted, and her back was turned to Avery as she rifled through clothes, unable to see Avery's quick look of hurt as she glanced down at herself. "But I can find you something perfect! What's your favorite color?"

"Uh, green," Avery looked back up to watch Maria spring into action. The young woman clicked her tongue a few times before quickly pulling out different articles.

"I don't have a green tunic unfortunately, but I do have a green cloak you can have. Try this ensemble," Maria tossed clothes onto the floor before dashing out of the room. "I'll watch the door for you!"

She looked at Maria's short stature in the doorway and was skeptical she could prevent any men from peeking if they had really wanted to. Her clothes were quickly shed, and she pulled on the milky-colored tunic. The black pants were loose on her legs, and she frowned. To have such a strong build would be so much better, anything to make her less of a girl and more of a woman her age. To be made more capable, particularly in her unusual situation.

Avery picked up the emerald cloak, fumbling in a tangle of cloth as she tried to put it on correctly. After she finally wrapped it around her shoulders the right way, she closed the swirling brass clasp that would sit comfortably at her clavicle. The material was quite thick to be wearing in the tail end of summer but it was simply too beautiful for Avery to put back into the bureau.

"Alright, it's on."

Maria whirled around to look, and her face lit up as she clapped her hands together once at her chest. "I like that on you far better than on me!"

Avery gave a skeptical smirk before looking away. Did she traverse through the forest for a week in order to be this woman's dress up doll? She wasn't sure if it was infantilizing or helpful; perhaps a little of both. Maria spoke again before she could shrug off the comment.

"Moz is going to take you into town to get armor, I can't exactly loan you that because it has to fit properly. I think he's out front waiting."

She whirled around and left the doorway, and when Avery stepped out of the room she had vanished. At the foot of the table Aegis sat on his haunches with a swishing tail.

"Well, she's a woman of many words. I thought she would never hush."

Instead of laughing like she wanted to, she shot the cat a scolding glare. "Now be nice, it's only to help."

"Why chide me? You were thinking it too," he slunk away towards the front door, his tail curling around the edge of the wood before disappearing. She pushed open the door, following the cat outside. He walked with his small body brushing against the wood of the siding before slinking around the corner.

"Aegis, where are you-SHIT!"

Avery yelped in startle, not expecting the tall figure to be directly on the other side. Moz was barely recognizable in his changed attire and from a quick glance he had become a black form. A black leather armor pad was strapped to his chest over a black shirt, though the sleeves had been hidden under a black coat that was tattered on the edges. Knives were strapped to his outer thighs over black pants. Yet he still wore his scuffed black boots from their journey.

Around his neck was a wide black cloth that would perhaps serve to cover his face, and a silent bell hung around a red cord. The symbol of Ara had been silenced presumably by removing the metal clapper on the inside. Avery had not expected an act of devotion from Moz as he had proven to be skeptical about everything.

"Don't you think that's overkill?" He seemed ready to assassinate the king rather than a simple trip into the nearest town.

He shrugged. "Say what you will, but any Knights of Od you encounter aren't going to wait until you're ready."

He began stalking off without her in the direction from which dark clouds began to roll in. Aegis followed him at a trotting pace and seemed more focused on the rat perched on Moz's shoulder. She frowned and followed them towards town.

— ❦ —

The small bell chimed behind Moz and though his instinct was to snap around in reaction, he knew it was only Avery. He glanced over his shoulder to see her tugging the brown leather plate on her torso from the bottom seam with obvious discomfort. She had a lot to get used to if that plate was even going to help.

Avery held out the black velvet bag he had handed to her in order to purchase it, and he snatched it with slight haste to open it to see what contents remained. He grimaced when his hand bobbed with the unexpectedly light weight and peered inside.

"Damn, Margot really put a dent in our funds."

When he looked up, he saw the blood had drained from Avery's face. She looked down at the plate and then back up at him.

"Is that bad? Should we give it back?"

He shook his head, swallowing down what was almost a chuckle. Even he wasn't proud enough to walk around without armor. "We can't cross the continent without armor. But we also can't without gold. We'll have to find another way."

Moz reached into a pocket on his left leg and pulled out a hard, leather container. He plucked one of the hand-rolled cigarettes and lit it while it was held between his teeth. The seductive darkness in the back of his skull laughed. He slammed the door in the demon's face and it was as though he heard the Knight clawing against his cerebellum.

"You're gonna have to be faster than that, Mozzy."

He ignored the demon and focused his attention back to the thinning crowd on the main avenue. If blood was not yet gushing out of his nose he would probably be fine - at least a little while longer. He watched the folds of women's dresses, the energetic twitching of a child's hands, and the slurred speech on the stained lips of drunken men all with sharp detail. Some were heading into their homes as the lanterns were being lit along the streets, and others were merely getting started with their boisterous nights. Though he watched for a long moment from where he stood under the guise of a smoke break, nothing called to him quite yet.

"Moz, shouldn't we go?"

Avery's voice quivered with nervousness, perhaps at the sight of the black orbs that began to bob out from between the shops. Though they had nowhere near the quantity of the swarm in Ardua, her reaction was to be expected.

"Just be quiet for a moment, will you?" He snapped with unintentional agitation as the nearly-empty sack began to feel heavier and heavier with the pressure of filling it. Instantly, he regretted his sharp tone.

Moz did not resort to picking pockets or any other form of theft very often. Any money he came across was typically done through mundane jobs that others would rather not do. Carcass removal, field plowing, courier services. Sometimes the money was obtained through dirtier and bloodier means; though every piece went towards tracking other Knights of Od and clashing against them. The money he stole from other people was, in a way, going back to them through protection. That wasn't so bad, right?

"Master, over there!" Jack had been perched on his shoulder, and he lifted a tiny pink paw towards a man across the avenue.

Moz caught sight of him just as he was placing a satchet inside his coat pocket. The brown beard on his face was scraggly and hung to his clavicle, his clothing equally grubby. He recognized the man from around town, though the places he spotted him always gravitated around one of the three taverns in town. This would be embarrassingly easy.

"This way, Avery," he instructed and continued down the avenue. He heard a shuffling of boots as she hurried to follow with Aegis padding alongside her.

The man wandered aimlessly in front of the shops; he wasn't quite sure what he was looking for and Moz began to do the same. Moz moved towards his target slower than he had crossing the avenue and he took his time glancing into windows of curiosity shops, careful to not arouse suspicion. Avery was looking at him with wild confusion, though he did not acknowledge it.

"You're right, I do think Maria would prefer a red cloak as opposed to another purple one. We might be able to look in some shops last minute or come back tomorrow," he began to speak to Avery as though they had been carrying a conversation as they approached the man. As he bent to examine the contents in a window, he glanced over his shoulder with a biting look to let her know to play along.

"Oh, um, I guess."

He rolled his eyes and straightened back up. Clearly she wasn't going to assist with this one.

Moz pretended to gaze distractedly as he walked, finally bumping the man in the side. His arms were just long enough to reach into the pocket of his jacket to lift the pouch and place it in his own in the confusion. The man spun around in shock, the sharp bite of whiskey hitting Moz's nose as soon as they were face to face.

"I'm incredibly sorry! Are you alright?" he feigned an apology. The man hiccupped and grinned with rosy cheeks, though he did not speak.

Moz patted him gently on the back and did his best to appear sincere. "Well, carry on sir. Cheers!"

He began to continue along the avenue in the direction they had been headed rather than behind them towards home. Simply too easy; though he could practically feel the tangible disgust radiating from Avery behind him as they walked away from the theft. Just when he thought they were home free, he heard a holler from behind them.

"Maurice, the man just pocketed ya!"

This voice was sober.

"Damn..." he hissed quietly to himself but kept walking, seeing if he could simply pretend he did not know what the man was talking about.

How did he miss the group of men across the street, who had a perfect view of what just happened? He had been careless and clumsy. The pounding of feet behind them led him to believe it was a group of four, perhaps friends of the man he had just robbed.

Moz finally stopped and turned around. Avery had frozen in fright a few paces behind him, Aegis stood at her feet with a rigid body to pounce on anyone who threatened her.

"I should have known… I've seen ya around and ya look of nothing but trouble," the tallest of the men snapped. The man's clothing was just as worn and dirty as Maurice's and his accomplices wore sinister grins. The man pushed back his coat to reveal the sword sheath attached to his hip to casually threaten Moz. Moz did everything in his power to avoid snickering at the pathetic display, though the sudden snarls from the men indicated he had not done too well.

"How about yer wife come with us, eye for an eye."

This time he didn't bother trying to stifle his laughter. "My wife?"

Moz expected Avery to turn around and shoot him an icy stare as soon as he had said it, but she stood frozen with terror between him and the other men. He looked at Hemlock strapped to her back and remembered that somewhere in the air around them stood a malevolent spirit only she could see. So far it had proved to work to her advantage when Owen had knocked Moz's sword right out of his grip, but could she stand up to four unsavory men? It could prove to be beneficial if she had any chance against Morgana's forces, or even the other Knights.

He stepped back two paces. "You know, I trust you to take care of them yourself."

That time she did turn around and look at him with wide eyes of horror before turning back to the men and shuffling backwards.

"Leavin' his whore to the dogs?" one of the men reached out and yanked Avery by her long hair, pulling her towards them and she buckled forward under the sudden force. Moz whistled in a decrescendo.

"That was a mistake," Moz commented.

Not even a moment after he spoke the words, a wooden crate flew from the shop front and crashed violently into the man's side. Enter a malevolent Owen.

The man let go of Avery's hair as he was knocked down by the force of the flying crate and she stood upright. Moz stepped around to view the confrontation from the side to gauge Avery's capability and intervene if the men pulled dirty tricks again. The men cried out in surprise and flailed about as they searched for the source of the flying crate.

The man who had flaunted his sword snarled as though he took Avery's threat as a challenge. When one of his comrades attempted to flee, the man grabbed him by the shirt and thrust him in Avery's direction. Avery ducked out of the way, her right arm reaching behind her to unsheathe Hemlock in a fluid motion. It grazed over her palm like a bow over a fine cello before she held it skyward in front of her.

The sword blinked its golden eye and their faces twisted with sheer horror. Their nightmares were realized even further when Moz became sure that they could also see the semi-transparent shadows seeping upwards from the dirt road beneath their feet. A ribbon of blood trickled down Avery's wrist and into her sleeve as she held Hemlock in front of her. Her eyes fogged over white as she stepped half-way into the realm of the dead, as Balthazar put it.

"I am nobody's wife. I am nobody's whore. If you dare to touch me again, I will snap you like a twig," her warm voice had grown as cold as ice and as sharp as glass, sending cold static up even Moz's neck - was this still Avery?

"A witch!" one of the men shrieked, stumbling backwards in reaction to her suddenly dark demeanor.

The shadows snapped forward at once, clawing at the men. Blood was drawn on the skin where Moz had expected their airy hands to simply pass over them. His eyes widened with sudden alarm. Shallow cuts appeared on their cheeks and hands as they gripped their swords harder, unsure of where to swing them.

"Avery, you need to stop!"

These men may have acted like scum, but they certainly did not deserve to be brutalized the way he was anticipating. Avery didn't budge and her spirits continued their assault. The long waves of her hair floated upwards and the spirit glass around her neck unburied itself from under her cloak to levitate toward the heavens. The men tripped over one another before fleeing and the shadows allowed them to flee only after they had put many yards between themselves and Avery. Their black forms slithered like snakes around Avery, wary of the men returning before the revenants vanished.

Her hair fell to her back and the chain of her spirit glass clinked against her cloak clasp as it returned to its place against her sternum. Hemlock slipped from her hand and fell to the ground with a blood-soaked grip before Avery collapsed backwards into the dirt. Aegis, who had been watching from the sideline as well, darted to her side with a twitching nose and traced her left side from her hip to her head.

Avery didn't respond in any way; the spirits had drained her of any energy in order to carry out their assault. Aegis then sat back, looking up at Moz as though he expected something.

"She'll get it eventually," he said to Aegis, picking up her sword and turned her slightly onto her stomach to sheath it for her. Grabbing her left arm and waist, he picked Avery up and slung her onto his back sideways.

"A little warning, Master!" Jack squeaked from his shoulder as he skittered down Moz's ribs and into a rat-sized pocket on his waist.

"I'll certainly remember to next time," he agreed. "We need to get back, hopefully she'll be alright before Alice and Kurosaki return."

They started on the road back to the shack, more sluggish than they were when they had arrived into town. With each step, Avery's limp arms hit Moz in the ribs as they draped in front of him to hold her up. Yet there was no sign of the cause, Owen, anywhere. Moz made a mental note to warn Tristan to banish the spirit; he had a feeling that he wouldn't require much convincing after hearing about this latest incident.

Aegis jumped from the fallen tree he had been walking along and into Moz's path as though to stop him, tail swishing.

"How much longer are you going to pretend you cannot hear me?" his low voice was as clear as the voice of the rat.

"What do you want, kitty?" Moz neither stopped nor slowed his pace. He had been ignoring the cat's jabs to Avery about him and was not about to give him another opportunity.

"What I want is to know why you can hear me," he demanded. *"You're not in the body of a cute house animal, which tells me you're not second class. You're a bigger demon."*

Moz made no indication of whether or not Aegis was right or wrong, but continued walking towards the glowing windows of their shack.

"Balthazar knows you personally and you should not be able to hear me if I'm not your spirit guide, therefore you can because you are a demon. Or have one. If you really are a Reaper like you say you are, then that can only mean one thing."

He felt rage flare up in the pit of his belly and stopped to stare at the cat with furrowed brows. Moz couldn't wait for Aegis to ditch the feline body so he could kick the shit out of the demon.

"What does that mean?" He dared Aegis through gritted teeth.

"You're one of the Beldam's Knights."

A blade slid loose from Moz's sleeve and he gripped it tight. "Give me one good reason not to skin you right here."

"Because I'm not going to tell my Mistress. Not yet. I want them gone as much as you do. If Avery knew, she would run from you. She's too trusting, but she's no idiot. You need her more than she needs you."

With that, the cat slinked off into the tall grass and disappeared. He stood still for a moment, too dumbfounded to move. What Aegis spoke was true, though putting it to words stung him bitter and cold.

The High Priestess sent him after Avery specifically as if he couldn't carry out his duties without her. His anger flared even hotter with the realization. He should never have to depend on anyone to do his job, necromancer or not.

CHAPTER SEVEN
THE LOVERS

Avery's stomach turned when she opened her eyes. What was she looking at? Her head ached as she tried to adjust her eyes to the dim setting. The firm surface under her arm told her she was on the ground laying sideways. Wood planks? Her dizzy gaze shifted up to see a pair of folded legs clothed in brown pants. In front of her was a small table that she had been lying partially beneath. She moved the hand that stung with idleness out from between her head and a pillow to rub her eyes.

"She's awake!"

The legs had belonged to Maria, who bent forwards to peek at Avery. "Are you alright?"

Her voice was soft and heavy with worry, a far cry from her bubbling giddiness upon meeting Avery. She sat up with a woozy head and her eyes strained to adjust on her surroundings. Shank sat across the table from her and was the first face to come into focus. Their face slowly transformed from stern worry to a smile of relief.

"Moz told us what happened," a different voice spoke from the corner. She lazily turned her head to see Tristan in a chair with a solemn expression. Ina stirred at his feet from the sudden deep voice. "Do y' remember anything?"

The images of the sudden swarm of people flooded her memory and the smears of blood from swiping the foul men. Though he wasn't present, she had remembered feeling Balthazar steering her through the whole event with both hands on her shoulders. The way Owen had lashed out was far more violent than Avery could have ever imagined, his small mouth snarled and golden eyes darkened by something she had pushed away out of fear.

Avery turned her head to look around the room slowly as if any sudden movement would set the spirit off again. Her stomach did somersaults when a swarm of black clouded her vision and rattled her skull. Avery slid backwards on her hands to get away, hoping it would lessen the effects. Another Reaper? Though she had experienced this sensation several times now, the nausea never became any easier to deal with.

The fog faded and warped until a pale, gentle face came into view. She looked deceptively young with lavender hair pulled up into two balls on the sides of her head. Her eyes were stormy grey pits and looked at Avery with dull wonder as she waited for the fog around Avery's face to fade before making any kind of an introduction. Wrapped around her elbow was the tail end of a dark brown serpent, the body slinking up her arm and behind her shoulders. Its head had traveled all the way down her other arm and stood upright, examining Avery with beady black eyes. Had she not seen the black fog around her face first, she might have fled in fear. Avery tried not to remind herself of what happened with Maria's familiar.

"Ave, this is Alice," Maria introduced her with a careful volume. "She's a friend who travels with Kurosaki."

"I don't know who that is," she whispered quietly, realizing as soon as she finished her sentence that Maria had already known that. She nudged her head towards the other end of the table with a bob of her short, dark hair. Moz had been seated at Avery's right side, unusually calm as a stream of smoke flared from his nostrils. Past him was another new face.

Everything about the man was pale except for his brown eyes. His hair was an ice blonde except where it grew in black at his scalp. A fur-trimmed hood in the tail-end of summer? His companion had been dressed just as strangely, clad head to toe in black and countless buckles and straps on her pants. Avery's eyes widened when she noticed the jarring difference between them.

"You're not a Reaper?"

"Well shit," it was not the man who spoke, but Moz. He stamped out his clove tobacco and stood up, leaving no one between her and the pale man.

"Was," the man stated simply.

Avery's eyes widened with intrigue. Was a Reaper? How could someone possibly be a former Reaper? She had been certain that being a Reaper was a condition to bear for eternity; or at least until she was struck down and died.

"But... how?"

He smiled the way a person would when their favorite topic is casually mentioned and they knew they were about to unleash a tsunami of information.

"The magic word: Saved. A Reaper can be relieved of their duties and guaranteed the gods' good graces if they can do one thing."

"And what's that?"

He looked down at her with his head tilted up, peeking out from under his eyelids. "What's your name? Avery, right? Would you say that you are a whole person?"

She flinched, baffled by his question. "What kind of question is that? Of course I am!"

"That's where you are wrong. When I was born into Reaperdom, I wasn't all of Izaya Kurosaki. Maybe eighty or ninety percent Kurosaki, but certainly not whole. This was because there was a certain emotion I was missing, something I struggled to grasp in my previous life. The Beldam made us, all of us, without that singular feeling. Because it would be real funny to make us try to find it, right? Something to bide our time so we don't worry about the Knights. Then I became a whole Kurosaki. No more notebook, no more fear of damnation. You're not a whole Avery. She's not a whole Alice, and he's not a whole William Mosley."

Avery's eyes traveled to Maria as though she would deny this to be true. She only stared back with reflective eyes and waited Avery's reaction. Avery turned back to Kurosaki.

"How did you do it?"

"It's pretty close to impossible to jump-start something like that on your own and it's often spurred by an outside event or person. In this case, it was Moz. I had my ass handed to me and that's how I first felt humility."

Moz? If he had helped this man be Saved, then there was no doubt that he had known about the missing emotions. She looked over her shoulder towards where he stood in the kitchen and it suddenly made sense that he would slink away from the conversation like he did.

"You knew? And you didn't say anything?"

"Wasn't my vote."

Avery rose to her feet the same way the anger boiled in her throat, climbing to her voice. "There was a vote? To not tell me? Who made that decision?"

The room was silent for a long moment and she heard only the pounding of blood behind her ears as her rage heightened. No one answered. Maria visibly swallowed hard in nervousness as she opened her mouth to speak and then closed it again. Another pause and she finally spoke.

"We had assumed Moz or Tristan had already told you in the forest. Shank and I had no idea, Ave."

Then that could only mean…

"Fuck you!" A cup violently flew off the table, crashing against the wall next to Tristan's head. She saw Owen's eyes alight with rage as he dragged a chair across the floor and Tristan shot up with a startled yelp. Owen laughed with satisfaction in the rise he got out of the large man. Maria shrieked and jumped up, swearing.

"Fuck, Moz! I believe you now!"

The small sound she heard next silenced the commotion. It was but a small click and when Avery turned her head she found herself staring down the barrel of a handgun. Behind it was Alice, her expression solemn and void of any light it held upon Avery's first look at the woman. A gun? She could have only been from Eyon; the city in the sea that watched from a quiet distance, secluded from the rest of the world.

"Lashing out with violence isn't going to make you any less afraid, hun," she cooed.

Only Avery was able to see Owen attempt to wrestle the firearm out of her hand, and it wobbled in Alice's fingers as her eyes widened with confusion. The holster on Alice's hip was quickly emptied as he dumped out the gun with his other hand.

Kurosaki quickly intervened, shoving Avery hard and she crashed into the wall behind her, sending a decorative arrow clattering to the floor. Blood dripped from her busted bottom lip as she hit the floor and she smeared it across her cheek with the back of her hand, standing up. Before the situation could escalate any further, Ina sat up rigid and alert with her ears erect. Everyone fell into a silent tension before Shank spoke.

"Something's out there."

The room erupted into a panicked hurry, each Reaper grabbing their bows and swords while Avery blinked with confusion. She followed them outside into the darkness that was broken only by the dim light from behind the colored windows. Her eyes adjusted slowly to the hills that surrounded them and for a moment she swore she saw a quick shape graze the horizon.

"SHOOT THE FUCKER DOWN!" Moz howled. Her eyes had not deceived her; the shriek of a peregrine answered, taunting Moz's command.

Maria was the first to snap into action, her left knee bending slightly in front of her as she pulled an arrow backwards in her bow. She followed the shape in the sky, entering and leaving visibility at random intervals in the patchy night sky.

"It's just the bird, y'reckon?" Avery heard Tristan's voice but could not see him.

"I doubt Morgana tailed us that fast," the grit of Moz's teeth was tangible in his voice. The bird shrieked again and the arrow Maria launched whistled through the air before missing its target. She swore and loaded another arrow as Shank fired their first, also coming up short.

The bird disappeared for the final time and all was still. Moz then swore violently and Maria lowered her bow.

"I don't know what you expected, we're literally shooting blind," she snapped defensively. Moz stood still with one hand waiting at the hilt of his sword on his side. Still waiting.

"Everyone rests now," he ordered in a low voice. "They're not here, but they're not going to wait. Morgana must have already had a squad near central Shintori."

He turned and stormed back into the shack, his cloak whipping behind him. Maria grabbed Avery by the hand and pulled her inside. "Let's clean that up and get some sleep."

Avery sat on a floor cushion, blood dribbling down her chin while Maria fetched a bowl of water. When she returned, Avery ripped off a small piece of her own shirt hem just like Tristan had shown her and dabbed it on her wound with water.

When the bleeding was finally staunched, Maria took Avery by the arm and led her to the back room where she had received her change of clothes earlier that day. The entire time she never uttered a word, and Avery found she preferred it to being patronized. When she was out of view from the main room Maria began removing her clothes to change. Avery quickly looked the other way with flushed cheeks. She wasn't certain if she should have disclosed the equal attraction she felt toward the same gender as she did toward others.

"I don't mind sharing my mat," Maria offered as she finished pulling on the shift and laid down on the side of the mat rolled out on the floor.

Avery hesitated before taking off her boots and sank onto the empty space on Maria's left side "Thanks… I didn't realize how aching my bones were until I stopped to rest," she laughed slightly as she tried to cut through the tension that only she seemed to be feeling. Maria chuckled as well, before silence fell over them for a brief moment.

"You wanna know something?" she asked in a quieter tone. Without giving Avery a chance to answer, she confided "Moz and I used to be together."

Avery turned her head and watched Maria as she spoke, barely seeing her face as Maria thought of an earlier time. She had absolutely no interest in the statement, but listened anyway.

"It was great in the beginning, and I think it might have been love. I guess I have no way of knowing. But something kind of stopped working, you know? There was no fight, no shouting, and no violence. Just one day we fell out. I think we might have realized it was only for the sake of finding out if one of our hidden emotions was love."

"That's awful, I'm really sorry," Avery whispered, doing her best to sound sympathetic. She tried to imagine them in an embrace or speaking sweetly to each other, but couldn't.

"No, it's not like that at all. There's sincerely nothing harsh between us. I think it's much better this way, honestly. I kind of see it as a small reminder that people like us are capable of such a thing.… Sometimes I forget that. I wouldn't have it any other way. You're gonna find your missing emotion, Ave… don't you worry.… "

Avery watched her face for a long moment, trying to find anything in her expression to contradict what she was saying. A glitter of hurt in her eyes, maybe the corners of her mouth turning down. Avery found nothing. She could have even sworn she saw a hint of a smile come across her full lips. It wasn't long until Maria's breath had grown soft and slow, falling rapidly into a slumber.

She tried to find any hint of Lily in Maria but she came up short. Maria was not perceptive to the fear and confusion Avery harbored that she knew her best friend would have detected immediately. This woman's eagerness did not match the slick caution exhibited by the cunning medical student. Where was Lily at that very moment? Worry gnawed in her ribcage like maggots eating their way to the surface and she failed to convince herself that Morgana's underlings had simply left Lily alone.

Hours passed as she listened to the footsteps and the padding paws in the main room dwindle to silence. Her vision began to grow blurry, dark exhaustion seeping in at the edges until all was black.

Lily had stopped pacing since her conversation with Iggy and Peter. Whether it was out of worry for Avery or that Morgana's eerie grin would be imprinted on her dreams, she was sure of nothing besides the fact sleep would not come easily. On occasion she would pause her anxious steps to look at the woman, illuminated by lanterns hanging from the lowest beams. They somehow made her look even bonier, as though her skin was merely shrink-wrap around her skull. Morgana would always catch Lily's stare, prompting her to resume pacing.

Every now and then she would stop to observe an animal passing by, most often a form of snake or large dog. These weren't the kind of animals you would take on board for slaughter, she was certain of that. So why were they there? Perhaps the hounds to pick up the scent of the murderers, the men who had her best friend captive. Lily tried to analyze the colors and patterns of the snake passing by to determine if it was venomous, though she audibly sighed with defeat when she had to admit to herself she knew nothing about reptiles.

In any other circumstance she would have cried out in fear, but the way the officers on board had neglected to point out their blatant presence made Lily feel it was their intent for the serpents to roam freely. Was it possible they were venomous and kept as a torture tactic for the criminals? Why not keep them contained?

"Morbid," she finished the thought out loud as she looked over the side of the deck before turning on her heel for what must have been the thousandth time.

The bird was only detectable in the dead of night by its piercing shriek. She turned to look down at the deck and saw Morgana jump out of her seat at the base of the main mast. The woman hurried to the port side, her arm held out once more to allow for the bird's return. The bird landed swiftly onto Morgana's arm, the captain swaying her limb back to roll with the force of the landing. With the peregrine falcon back in place, Morgana's grimace eased to an expression of relief.

"Peter!" she called out hastily.

His spectacles reflected a flash of light as he poked his head around the helm, though she didn't wait for an answer from her subordinate before continuing.

"They've been spotted in Centralia and Sera's battalion is on the move. We approach from the west to prevent them from moving into the next town if they evade her," she barked hurriedly. "He says there are two from Eyon, one is a Saved. Avery Porter is there, unharmed."

Lily's eyes widened at the sound of her friend's name. She flew down the steps to the deck Morgana occupied, feeling a bizarre eagerness to speak to her.

"Thank Ara, she's unharmed! Who saved who, does that mean you have troops there already?"

"Though she is unharmed now, I fear that with the criminal alliances manifesting, she is not safe for much longer," Morgana's velvet voice had turned cold.

She turned sharply on her boot heel and walked in the other direction to leave Lily in her own fear. She shrunk back and fled down to the lower deck. Pushing past officers and prompting gruff complaints, she sought out the darkest corner she could hide in. Past the galley and past another ladder, she found a space set aside for storage that was filled with stacked crates. She burrowed between two wooden towers and sank to the floor.

Her hands gripped her knees tightly with aching knuckles. She willed herself to calm her breathing out of fear for both passing out and for drawing attention to herself. After all, there were only so many places to hide while at sea. Her eyelids fluttered shut and she tried to imagine herself curled on the ragged couch at home. She tried to imagine the warmth of the lamp light, the smell of dark brewed coffee. The gentle crinkle of Avery turning a page in her book, the pad of Aegis' small paws on the floor boards. It was all within her reach it seemed, but it was not there.

What would her brother think if he knew where she was? Byron would surely have a heart attack if he knew the danger his baby sisters were in. He would also know what to do, his survival skills far surpassed hers. No matter how much she wanted to believe that she was independent, she knew she was sheltered. What would Byron do?

"Are you going to be okay?" Her thoughts were interrupted by a man's voice.

She looked up and met Peter's gaze, his glasses farther down on his nose than they should have been and his face painted with worry.

"I... I guess I'm just overwhelmed," she was only slightly feigning. "Now that we know she's alive, I don't know how I'm going to fight to get Avery back."

Peter crouched down so he could speak and be at her eye level. Though she knew he probably meant to be comforting, she felt like a patronized child.

"Don't fret about the fighting part of it, we'll take care of that. We just need you to convince Miss Porter she's safe to come with us."

A small sliver of Lily doubted she was, but Morgana's creepiness was undoubtedly better than being in the hands of murderers. She had seen Avery's look of terror even as she followed the men, they had some kind of hold over her; but how? Why did Avery even go with them in the first place if it was safe to come with the police?

Lily was the first to stand up and he straightened up to meet her. She brushed herself off more for show than for ridding herself of dust. "If you promise to protect both of us, I can do that."

Peter smiled, bright with sincerity. "I promise."

Avery was shaken hard, her eyes opening wide at once to see Shank kneeling in front of the mat. They were frowning as they rattled her by the shoulders and then all at once their expression lit up with satisfaction upon her awakening. Shank removed their hands and put them on their crouched knees.

"I thought for a moment you might have been dead! Heavy sleeper, aren't we?"

She didn't answer, but propped herself up on one elbow and looked around in a daze as she tried to gather her surroundings. Maria was already gone from the room and her voice could be heard among the ones floating in from outside. Shank didn't give her time to ask what was going on.

"You have just enough time to feed yourself and Aegis before we go," even though their speaking was hurried, it seemed like they were making a conscious effort to be friendly to her. "There's bread and milk left on the table for you. We need to head to the temple as soon as we can."

Her eyes were heavy with grogginess from her sudden awakening. Shank was already leaving the room before she could ask any further questions. She sat up on the mat, rubbing the sleep out of her eyes. Hemlock was laid to the side in a web of straps and Aegis made careful steps through it to avoid getting caught.

Avery shook her head and stood up, the brief dizziness passing after mere seconds. After she replaced her leather chest plate and sword sheath, she scooped the cat into her arms and floated into the main room for food.

"—but I'll be the one to talk to them. You and Maria will stay fanned out and keep an eye out for anyone who may be affiliated with the Knights," Moz's voice trailed inside from the huddle of Reapers outside the window.

"I'm not sure yet where Avery will be best suited, so she'll come with Tristan and myself into the inner walls of the temple grounds."

"Where do you want me and Kurosaki?"

"Alice and Kurosaki," Moz continued, and any doubts Avery had about who was leading this plan had diminished; it was clear he had considered this countless times. "As usual, never fire any bullets unless one of our lives is immediately threatened. Assume hiding points to snipe when you see Sera, Morgana, or Peter. When you must intervene, your go-to should be your blades. Conserve what little ammo from Eyon you have. Your first priority is to watch over Maria and Shank outside the walls. Send Mori out to Ina if you need to warn them. Should the situation change, I trust your judgement."

"Would Mori even be fast enough? The Priestess is going to draw a crowd," Alice replied.

Maria chimed in next. "I don't know about all of you, but if I suddenly saw a snake Mori's size slithering around my feet, I would clear out of the way pretty fast. Besides, she doesn't need to go far. Just within range for Ina to hear."

Avery walked to the door quietly to join the conversation, but also waiting to see if anything would be mentioned that she was not supposed to hear.

"Precisely," Moz confirmed. "We'll have Aegis and Jack on the inside. You can come outside, Avery."

He hadn't missed a beat in noticing her. Avery poked her head around the door frame before stepping into full view. Her eyebrows furrowed. "How did you know I was here?"

Moz simply nodded his head downward towards her feet and she followed the gesture to see Jack sitting up on his hind feet, gazing up at her with black beads.

"Nobody can out-stealth Mozzarella here," Alice joked and Moz pulled a hard frown at the nickname. Avery joined them and noticed Owen blending into their group, his expression eerily calm.

"Except for me, perhaps," he said in rebuttal to Alice's claim but there was no challenge. His arms folded across his chest and Avery felt a pang of sorrow for the boy. How sad it must have been to be surrounded by people but never acknowledged.

So she relayed "Owen would like to protest that statement."

Maria snickered while Alice looked confused. "Who?"

As Tristan explained their invisible ally, Avery trailed behind Moz as he walked out to the shanty stable that Maria had pointed out the day before. Though he did not say anything she knew that he was already aware of her presence. He pulled the sliding door open with both hands and thrust it open. When she followed him inside she stopped in her tracks in the frame of the door.

There was no way she could have missed the black titan. The light that flooded in through empty windows reflected no color in its eyes as it watched Moz approach. She remained gaping at the horse when the other Reapers entered the stable.

He ignored her astonished reaction as he led the horse out by its reins. "Find someone else to ride with, Emory doesn't like most people."

To her right, Kurosaki was saddling a horse the shade of autumn oak and Alice tapped her foot impatiently as she waited to mount behind him. Maria, however, was working with Shank hurriedly as she climbed on the large white horse to sit at the front of the saddle. Avery turned to Tristan, who was preparing a black horse far less threatening than the one belonging to Moz.

"I need to get Aegis first," she said and hurried out, though she received no indication the exorcist had been listening. She collected the cat and after an internal debate, decided it would be best if he rode within a saddle bag. After placing him on top of the old t-shirt she had stuffed inside, she used the creaky wooden stall bars to climb onto the horse behind Tristan.

"Are y' scared?"

Avery had not noticed her shaking hands until he posed the question and she looked down at her wobbling knuckles. Though none of the Reapers had said explicitly that there would be battle, she knew it from their sense of urgency and extra weapons strapped to their persons. Avery fumbled with her hands in attempt to lock her arms around Tristan to hold on as they left the stall, the powerful equestrian hips shifting beneath her.

"Does it matter if I am?" she retorted instead of answering the question. Perhaps if she denied it, she could be brave. Tristan didn't answer and she had the feeling he knew better than to believe her. The horse jolted into motion and she squeezed her arms tighter around Tristan, instantly giving away her fear.

"Don't worry, the town's but a few miles away. Faster on horse than it was when ya and Moz walked."

She watched he grassy hills turn into a blur until the speed combined with how high she was off the ground dizzied Avery, and she put her face against Tristan's back.

Long minutes passed of Avery pleading mentally with the gods to spare her life before the horse slowed to a trot on the edge of Centralia. She cautiously looked away from Tristan's back, worried they might unexpectedly break into a sprint again.

Squat brick buildings came into view and the grass gave way to a dirt road tamped down by the feet of villagers and wheels of wagons passing through. The avenue was far more congested with people than there had been when Moz took Avery to get her armor; were they all here to see the Priestess too? Ardua had no temple and she could not compare the devotion of the village with that of the city.

They stopped outside of one of the first buildings, a tavern, with wooden beams built to waist height. Tristan's horse slowed to a stop under his command of the reins before he jumped off.

"Ya need help?"

Avery shook her head and swung her left leg over before jumping to the ground, the shock of the earth sending a painful vibration through her shins and seizing her knees before disappearing. Before he could whine in agitation, she reached in the saddlebag to retrieve Aegis. He promptly seized the opportunity to slash his feline claws on the back of her hand as his own brand of petty revenge and she fought every urge not to toss him onto the ground.

"You bastard!"

She set him down much more kindly than she would have liked to and Aegis only laughed before slinking away from the horses to pace around Ina's feet while she waited for the Reapers. Moz dismounted Emory with a heavy thud of his boots and he tied the horse to the beam.

"We travel in the groups we discussed earlier," he mumbled so lowly Avery wasn't sure she heard him quite correctly but she knew his intent was to be discreet. "Be vigilant and mindful of your surroundings. Avery and Tristan, follow me."

They tread into the town with Aegis catching up to them. As they walked Avery caught the stares of several people looming on the edges of the avenue. The irritation of the eyes didn't set in until the tenth or eleventh person who broke the gaze in a hurry.

"What the fuck is their deal," she snapped, looking at Tristan for an answer.

"They know what you did to Maurice and his goons last night," Moz was the one who spoke without looking back at her.

She halted. "What? We need to erase his memory or something! You can do that, right Tristan?"

"I can't and there's no point," Tristan shook his head. "Besides, the people here know a lot more than y'give em credit for. I hope y'don't take this personally, but Centralians aren't as out of touch with the gods as the people in Ardua; they know all the stories. They know about Beldam's Reapers and they know about Mona's witches. Even just lookin' around could tell y'how superstitious we are."

Avery resumed walking but glanced at each shop they passed. She had not noticed before the red strings hanging from the frames of shop doorways, small bells chiming with each swing of the door and parchment charms flapping in the warm breeze.

"They don't know specifically who is what," Moz added. "But I think it's safe to say you threw yourself out into the open."

"Shit," she hurried a few steps to follow closer to Moz, trusting his instincts more than she trusted hers.

"Shit is right. They may be aware but they're not as welcoming as Wrencrest."

"Wrencrest?"

"Ask Maria or Shank," he dodged the question with a shrug before making a clear end to the conversation by striding faster towards a large building at the head of the avenue.

The Temple stood tall at the far end of the town as a silent guardian, the white stone reflecting back every ounce of sunlight from the late summer sky. Four towers stood in the cardinal corners and loomed over the white wall standing between the town and the temple's insides. An iron-studded door of wood stood at the top of the white steps. Avery's gaze travelled upwards as Moz and Tristan already began to climb them.

"Make haste," Moz growled and she snapped upwards to follow.

Guards clad in metallic armor stood firmly on either side of the door. She mentally dared them to make any visible movement but they remained rigid at their post. When she reached the top step Tristan was already speaking with one of them, though she only caught the guard as he spoke.

"—informed that Her Holiness was indeed expecting you. You are permitted within the wall, you are not permitted into the Temple at this time."

The guard pulled out a bronze key from beneath his chest armor, turning it into the keyhole that had almost gone unnoticed in the massive door. Metal clanked and creaked as tumblers and plates shifted for a long moment, spanning across the entire door from the inside.

Tristan looked over his bulky shoulder to scan the town behind him, clearly wary of what he might find. She looked behind her as well. Though people had began to congregate in front of the temple stairs, nothing seemed out of the ordinary. Avery turned and followed the men inside.

Inside the walls laid a courtyard somehow even more pristine than the exterior of the temple grounds. White stone was arranged on the ground around a fountain in the center. Water gushed from the center of a stone lily and was fed back into the large pool around it. On the opposite side of the fountain was the façade of the temple itself, the porch lined with modest columns as white as ivory. Bells attached to red cords hung from each end of the colonnade and reminded Avery of the one hanging in her windowsill at home.

Before Avery could comment on the wondrous sight, the temple doors swung open. Two more guards emerged from the open mouth of the prayer hall, between them floated a figure dressed in heavy white robes. The only way Avery could tell it was a solid being and not a ghost was the way the sun was soaked up in the white canvas - the Priestess became a wondrous painting of light. At first her small footsteps made only short advances, her stride quickened to push past any formalities or displays she might have been obligated to observe.

"Mr. Mosley, Mr. Díomasaigh," she greeted the two men and gave Avery a warm smile without showing her teeth nor looking at her from under the white canvas hood. Her face was as pale as the moon with lips painted poppy red. "I am glad that they were able to find you."

"The information I have to disclose is of utmost secrecy, so please gather around," she advised. The trio leaned in closer so that the Priestess need only to whisper. Avery still doubted that security was an issue with how many guards were surrounding them.

"This Knight will be much more difficult to obtain than I had hoped," she whispered. "Our oracles found out that the last one was placed within the daughter of King Harthmoor, Yumi. They have already left the Neri Shrine in Eyon and make haste to Brightloch to see her for themselves, for we do not know if she resists the Beldam."

"What do you mean resisting," Avery asked. A creature designed for specifically havoc could simply resist? It sounded too good to be true.

"The Knights are demons that simply live within the selected Reapers, there is still a person inside who can fight and hold back the destruction. Willpower versus willpower. Though I fear that whoever harbors one will succumb eventually."

"What do we do once we find the Princess?" Tristan was bent forward slightly at the waist to hear her small voice carefully.

"Bring her to Eyon. On the southern cliffs you will find a stone sanctuary surrounding a pit. The pit is the mouth to the earth, and calls for blood from a Knight and blood from a Saved Reaper. I understand that you are acquainted with a Saved man already, is that correct?"

Avery turned to look at Moz, whose eyes were as wide as she had ever seen them and his voice cracked with relief when he murmured.

"It's that simple?"

She didn't answer his question and instead stated "That will surely end this unholy force forever. When you—"

The arrow was nothing more than a whistling past Avery's shoulder before blood bloomed in the Priestess' white robes, one of her own dark hairs was pinned between the weapon and the garment. An iridescent feather hung on the other end, tied by a jute cord. The Priestess' eyes widened with horror, looking at the weapon lodged in her flesh before turning up at the three travelers.

Bright purple veins snaked up her neck, crawling up her chin until they closed in on her face. The Priestess buckled at the knees, sinking down towards the floor before she toppled over. Tristan jerked forward, trying to keep her from falling but acted too late. She lay on her side, the blood seeping further across her garments.

Moz's fingers delicately reached down to touch the feather before he was shoved away by panicked guards.

"That arrow was poisoned and signed, I know who did this," he shouted to both Tristan and the guards who had separated them. Tristan's blonde hair was flying in all directions as he searched for the source of the arrow but it didn't take long for Moz to stop his scan.

"There," he growled. Avery whirled around until she was facing the direction Moz was pointing in.

Perched on the west wall was another figure hooded and cloaked in a shade of green much darker than Avery's. She caught only a glimpse before they stepped backwards off the wall with an alarming grace.

"Sera," Moz announced darkly. "Her guide is a gray wolf. Make sure—"

He stopped at the sound of shouting and clanging metal coming from outside the temple gates. Drawing his sword, he pointed it towards the door.

"AVERY, GO!"

Avery was startled by his shout but jumped into action. He actually trusted her enough to send her out first? She drew Hemlock before sprinting to the door with Aegis trailing behind her.

"Sera's accomplices are already upon Shank and Maria, we must assist them and take out her demon."

"Leave that to me," she answered him as she pushed open the gate. "Find Mori to pass on all the information we have."

Aegis immediately darted down the steps and his small body disappeared into the crowd. A black swarm hung over the front of the temple, uniformed and badged bodies beneath it. She found it baffling that so many Reapers were so willing to go along with the plans of Morgana and the Beldam, perhaps unaware of the consequences. Screams erupted when bodies fell at the Reapers' feet, the dead dressed in blood-soiled street clothing. The air left Avery's lungs violently as she realized what was happening. They were slaughtering everyone there for worship.

When the black haze had faded, many eyes were upon her. An Arduan officer who had yet to participate in the massacre drew his blade and stepped up towards her cautiously. Her heart pounded with the sudden confrontation and she held her sword crossed in front of her with one hand held out.

"Don't fail me now," she begged her sword out loud.

Avery dragged the edge of Hemlock across her palm, drawing warm blood until it dripped off of the hilt and onto the pristine stone. The seeing glass around her neck floated upwards as her eyes glazed over white. She had not seen the black orbs lying dormant just below the ground until her vision put her halfway into the realm of the dead and she entered just in time to see them emerge from the earth. Her hair floated as a tall shadow stretched up from behind her, blotting out the sun. She didn't have to turn to know it was Balthazar.

"KILL THE WITCH!"

The shout was blood-chilling and female. Avery turned towards the source and saw the figure perched on a rooftop several buildings away from her. Another poisonous arrow was drawn and this time she was the target. A flash of black closed in on Sera to slash with a sword, undoubtedly Moz, but not in time to stop Sera from releasing her arrow.

Avery waved her sword to the right, an anonymous spirit who had only moments ago been earthbound knocked it out of her path. Gratefulness flooded her and she hoped that somehow the revenant could sense it. She flinched, startled by the sudden flashing of arrows in her peripheral vision until she turned and realized they had come from Shank and Maria. They had remained hidden on the outskirts of the street, dressed in the shadows of the brownstone houses.

Avery quickly turned to face the gory crowd, just in time to see Alice holding two curved swords crossed on the throat on a uniformed woman.

"Off with your head!" Alice squealed with murderous glee and the woman was headless before she could scream. Avery's stomach turned and she stumbled, wanting to vomit.

"Don't forget what these people want to do," Balthazar's voice was somehow both calm and bone-rattling behind her. "It is more important to them to be on the side they perceive will win than to prevent the dead from bleeding into the land of the living. People you care about and people I care about are at risk."

People he cared about, as a demon? She looked over her shoulder at the demon of the crossroads and he grinned toothily back at her. Her bloody and sweaty grip on the hilt of her sword shifted before tightening. Avery turned back towards the mass, only to shriek in surprise at the sword swung at her. Crouching lower she swung Hemlock at the knees of the man attacking her. Though she made no contact, he backed away before the foggy spirits were upon him. Seizing the opportunity, Avery put all her weight behind her hips lurched upwards and severed the man at the throat.

Pins and needles pricked the flesh of her hand where she held Hemlock and she recalled Owen telling her about a blood sacrifice to the sword. Did that mean any blood at all, not just hers? The bronze eye on the hilt gently closed its leathery lids before blinking hard as the blood soaked into leather that wrapped the hilt. A tsunami of power washed over her, pulsing in every vein. Avery knew this power was not meant for her, it was intended for Paion; could she even contain it? Every hair stood on end and her nerve endings buzzed with electricity as Hemlock teemed with life in her clenched fist.

Rather than wait for the next of Morgana's legion to attack her first, she jumped into the fight with primal fury burning every inch of her flesh. She screamed with rage, setting her sights on the men that stood over bodies of villagers.

"The witch, she's a berserker!"

A berserker witch? She liked the sound of that. Her vision exploded with crimson petals as flesh was ripped, by her own doing. With a turn of her hand, the closest objects the spirits could find were thrown in the air like cannonballs. Crates, bricks, anything not nailed down to the ground became a merciless projectile. Splinters exploded and Avery ducked to avoid the shards of glass bottles they violently hurled. Only when they ran out of objects did their fingers start ripping at skin that Avery couldn't get to, and she remembered the words she exchanged with Maurice and his filthy dogs the night before. Her rage deepened and she slashed faster.

A foot kicked her hard in the stomach and broke the spell, sending Avery flying backwards into the ground. Hemlock clattered out of her fingers and she scrambled across the ground to reach it as the man who had attacked lunged at Avery. She screamed and kicked at him, the sole of her boot cracking against his jaw. He howled in rage and gripped her left leg with his free hand to drag her towards him. Where the fuck were the ghosts?

She screamed Owen's name as she rolled out of the way of the sword before it struck the earth. Her attacker stomped hard on her cloak to pin her down. He laughed disgustingly at the fear welling in Avery's eyes when she still could not reach her fallen weapon. Avery fumbled with the complicated clasp on her cloak, desperately trying to free herself. She couldn't give up, not like this.

All at once his chest exploded with gore and Avery shielded her eyes. When she felt the pull on her cloak released she looked up and saw Tristan retrieving his sword from the chest cavity of the attacker. He looked at her with his irritating jubilance.

"When ya' got the option, always pick the warriors o'er the dead guy."

She took Hemlock back into her bloodied hand and accepted Tristan's help to her feet with her other. On the other side of the fight she saw Moz disappear after Sera past the edge of the town, where the trees loomed over the tavern tops.

"We can follow them and pull the group into an area where they won't kill any other villagers," she advised. "Tell the others, I'll chase them."

She leapt into a run, making sure to avoid the bloody brawl from its outskirts. Before ducking with her into the alley, Avery's revenants made another assault on the skin of murderers, daring them to follow Avery. Their loud cursing and grunts followed close behind her as she ran and she knew she had baited them successfully. Behind her was the squish of metal passing through flesh, Tristan picked them off before they could close in on her.

Avery came to the edge of the trees and caught a glimpse of Sera's cloak before the assailant disappeared into the shadows. Anger sparked in her legs and she pushed faster only through sheer will. Female shouts echoed across the trees and held words that she couldn't decipher but the fury was clear as day.

Her breathing became labored heaving long before she even saw the clearing in the trees. When Avery reached its edge she crouched low to avoid being seen by the two figures standing static and facing each other from yards away. Why wasn't Moz ripping her apart? Was the low rumble his voice? What was he saying?

Sera's shorter form began pacing to try approaching Moz from a different angle and a higher mumble came from her voice as she answered him. Avery tightened her grip on Hemlock; if Moz wouldn't make a move, maybe it was up to her. Maybe he was counting on her to strike as he did only minutes before.

Slowly Avery crept forward and she worried a rain of arrows would pelt her as soon as she stepped out from under the safety of the forest canopy. She straightened her stride when she saw Sera's head peer past Moz's shoulder to catch sight of Avery's approach.

"Stay there!"

Moz had not even turned to yell the command and Sera's attention turned back to him as she lowered her hood to reveal a head of flaming hair. Her face was heavy with sympathy as she looked at Moz; finally her words came into earshot.

"We've given you every chance and more, William."

"So have I," he bit back.

Twigs cracked under approaching feet and the air around them snapped as a gunshot was fired off, the echo bouncing off the trunks of the trees before coming back to Avery's ears. She dropped her sword and covered her ears as the drums inside them rang, looking up to find the target. The bullet lodged itself in Sera's sternum, her armor visibly punctured. The woman stumbled backwards, her arm reaching behind her to brace her fall to the ground before she crashed into a heap in the grass.

Sera looked from the bloodless wound to Alice as she emerged from the dark tree line with her gun still held up and a disturbingly toothy grin spread across Sera's face. Behind Alice followed Shank and Maria, bows held armed and strong to escort in a blood-spattered Tristan.

Sera jammed a finger into the hole, pulling out the warped piece of metal with only a wince. Avery watched in horror as she dropped the bullet, her gray wolf stepping on it as it circled around Sera's feet without any regard to the gunshot.

"You think Beldam wouldn't put her Knights into the world without letting them fight?"

Sera unclasped her cloak, letting it fall to the dirt. Roots emerged from beneath her feet and wound around her legs as they turned an inky black. Moz quickly backpedaled, making room as though he knew exactly what was happening. Her spine lengthened as dark splotches began to dot her skin, and she let out a piercing cry of agony as she threw herself onto the ground on her hands and knees. Still the splotches appeared until a green sheen overcame her in leathery folds.

Sera burst violently and exposed bones stretched towards the sky to reveal a horrific creature, far beyond the strangeness Avery could create in her own mind. Avery scrambled backwards in horror, gripping Hemlock as tightly as she could bear to. Leathery wings unfurled from Sera's gigantic body, a beast's body, from exposed bones. She had become a titanic horse in an advanced state of decay - if horses had reptilian horns down their visible spine and the skeletal tail of an alligator.

The beast paced with a swishing tail as it waited for one of the Reapers to challenge it. She could not be sure if it was her imagination or not, but the demonic stare fell on Moz more than anyone else.

Kurosaki turned his gaze to Moz, leaving only a second before firing directly into his forehead. The force knocked Moz off his feet and Avery shrieked. He lay still on the ground and she was sure he would not rise. She held one hand over her mouth, stifling back the grief. Maria cried out, first for Moz before her cries thickened with rage around Kurosaki's name.

After a horribly long moment of shock, Moz's leg bent upwards off the ground as he struggled to lift himself up.

She had never seen such a look of burning contempt on his face before as he plucked the metal out of his brow, roaring in pain before discarding it. Blood dripped from his nostrils rather than the wound; gushing over his lip just as it had after meeting Balthazar.

"Izaya Kurosaki, you never fail to piss me off," he roared, blood spattering as it dribbled over his upper lip. "What the fuck would you have done if your theory was wrong?"

"But I was right. You're a Knight of Od."

She listened to their sharp tongues, firing off the way competitive brothers would while she was frozen in place. Avery couldn't take her eyes off of Moz, her bones frozen in place in a response to hide from the sudden danger. As he scanned his friends with eyes of rage and skimmed over her, she felt death were already upon her.

A Knight? He had lied to them the entire time; he was one of them.

Her vision blurred in intense fright and she held her breath as though it could prevent him from seeing her. He then turned his back to them, walking towards the sickly green beast awaiting him.

The ground did not envelop his ankles as it had to Sera, but Avery felt droplets of rain strike the top of her head. Those clouds had not been there moments ago, had they? When he crouched low, his skeleton exploded as Sera's did to allow the green Knight to emerge.

The dragon-like beast huffed heavily, its leathery skin tinted blue. In places there was no sapphire skin at all, only bones. The Knight's head was elongated and horse-like with two sharp horns forming at the brow. Its wings were mostly a bone frame with webs of flesh only in some places below the radius bone. They flexed outward before pulling back against its body, very much like a bat.

The thick bones of its legs leaned back and its tail swished, watching the emerald beast that challenged it. Thunder rumbled above their heads and the light rainfall became a downpour.

"He's the Knight of Water!" Shank shouted over the rain from the edge of the trees where they had retreated to. "He'll kill us all in a flood if we don't put him down NOW!"

Moz? He was a Knight. The fact still burned in her temples and she swayed with the dizzying effect it had. Moz, who roared with such hatred when he spoke of Morgana and the Beldam? It was him all along.

Shank's shout was reduced to a buzzing in her eardrums, the only sound Avery heard was the pounding within her ribs. Before she could backpedal away from the beast, she was running toward it for no discernable reason. The other Reapers behind her shouted her name to bring her back to them but it was as though she was pulled toward the Knight by an unseen chain. The giant's equestrian head turned toward her in a sharp black gaze and it was then that Avery heard the call of the demon as clear as a bell.

My witch.

— ❧ —

"Somebody stop her!" Maria pleaded, her voice cracking.

Yet even she stepped back after considering chasing Avery, knowing that she was no match for the Knights preparing for a fight. She looked at her friends for reassurance but even Shank's usual air of happiness had turned grim.

"I reckon the best thing we can do is stave off Sera," Tristan cautioned. "She'll be the one to definitely go after Ave. If we're lucky, Moz and his Knight will be too preoccupied to hurt her."

"She's climbing onto the Knight!" Shank pointed in the direction Avery had run. Maria's head whipped around and her eyes widened as she confirmed the bizarre sight. Avery was grabbing onto exposed rib bones to scale the side of the sapphire beast, Hemlock sheathed on her back.

"He's not even trying to shake her off," she murmured, looking down at Aegis near her feet and then back to the beast. She had expected Moz's Knight to violently thrash to throw off the small Reaper, but it did no such thing. If Maria didn't know any better, seemed the Knight wanted Avery to mount it.

"Ina says Aegis was pushed out of Avery's head. Something's in there blocking him," Shank said, their tone dark and stern. In front of them, Ina watched with tense muscles; pacing as though even she was debating whether or not to jump into the fray and save Avery.

Avery had mounted the Knight's back and the Knight of Water pounced on the other. Ear-splitting bellows echoed off the trunks of the trees and Alice was finally the first to spring into action.

"Shank, Maria, fire your arrows first at Sera's Knight to gauge its reaction. Kurosaki and I will fire rounds if need be. Tristan and Ina, look out for what's left of her backup forces. They should be closing in any second."

Shank and Maria looked at each other, nodding in agreement before hustling to the tree line for cover. She stuck close to a trunk as she reached behind her shoulder, pulling a feathered arrow from her quiver and placing it in her bow. As Maria held the bow in a position of rest she observed the fight unfolding before her.

"Avery's trying to slash at Sera from his back," Shank noted in a low voice as they watched. "I'm glad she's doing what she can… but he's just getting in our line too many times."

They were right; Moz's Knight made deep lunges for the green Knight's neck. His jaw snapped down with terrifying force but missed her quick dodges every time before backpedaling and trying again from a different angle. Avery had attempted to make cuts with Hemlock using only one hand but came up short and slashed at empty air when Sera evaded her jabs.

If Maria could distract the green Knight and give Moz's demon the tiniest window of time to attack, that would help them. Maria took a deep breath with squared shoulders, her right hand releasing. The arrow whistled through the air into the clearing, skimming past the emerald Knight's giant skull by a mere yard. Its attention turned towards the two archers for a second and that was all the time Moz's Knight needed to ram into it with furious force. Sera bellowed in pain, her leather wings flapped in deep sweeps and her fore legs lifted from the ground.

"Oh shit, now there's something we didn't plan for."

"I hope Avery's got a *reeeeeal* good grip there," Shank added. They fired more arrows to somehow keep the beast on the ground but they never made contact.

The green Knight launched into the air, the blue one shot upwards in pursuit and Avery's screams disappeared into the cloud cover.

— ❦ —

Avery felt nausea wash over her as the ground beneath them vanished into cloud, the cold wind dried her throat as she screamed. She sheathed Hemlock as quickly as she could in order to grip the exposed bone with both her hands, at any moment the wind could have whipped her off the flying beast to send her to a certain death.

"M...Moz! Moz! We need to get back to the ground NOW," she screamed, not entirely sure that he could hear her over the howling of the wind.

A flash of green soared through her periphery and Avery quickly turned her head to the left, catching a glimpse of the Knight of Od before her wet hair blocked her vision. She cursed and turned her face back forward while trusting Moz to pursue it. He let out a low, drawn-out growl before banking towards the other Knight. Avery's fingers clenched with white knuckles as she tightened her grip.

Moz was in close pursuit, the tail of his opponent swishing only yards away from the snout of his demonic form. Avery crouched as low against his body as she could to protect herself from the blast of the wind, peering past his long neck whenever she could.

"MOZ! If you can get close enough to her… I can get a shot at her!"

His giant head bowed and bobbed as though to approve and her eyes widened with shock. This whole time she had been stammering on to stave off fear, but he could understand her! How much of this beast was the demon? How much of it was still Moz? He angled his body upward and began to climb over the clouds. Avery swore at herself, angered by whatever drew her onto the Knight in the first place.

She squeezed her eyes shut as they rose higher and higher, her ears ringing as the pressure weighed on her eardrums. "I'm gonna die, I'm gonna die, I'm gonna die, I'm gonna…"

A blood-chilling roar split the air behind them and she opened her eyes to look over her shoulder. Her eyes widened at the sight of the Knight closing in on them. Avery hesitated to lift her left hand from the bony grip and grabbed Hemlock's handle as quickly as possible. She held it flat against Moz's spine in order to hold both the sword and the bone at the same time.

"Moz!" she called out, trying to coax him to make a move. The faster they could get back down to the ground, the better Avery's chance of surviving became.

Moz sharply banked to the left as Sera was about to make impact, Avery clutched the Knight's body as tightly as she could. Avery thrust out her sword only a second before they scraped against Sera's side, Hemlock's drag cut a long wound into the emerald Knight's ribs. Sera erupted in a sound unlike anything Avery had ever heard. The cacophony of pain and agony made her feel guilty - for only a fraction of a second.

Sera recoiled, trying to put as much distance between the beasts as she could before swiping at them. Moz swiftly evaded the initial attack but the Knight followed through much too quickly for him to dodge. Avery saw the gnashing teeth and her vision went white.

Death.

A loud roar erupted beneath her and Avery's heart went beating on. She opened her eyes and saw blood before her. A wound about half the size of Sera's open jaw was now open on Moz's left shoulder only inches from where she was. A dull burn in her arm grew brighter and brighter. Avery hissed and looked down at her left forearm. Her sleeve was ripped open and blood quickly seeped through the ivory fabric. The wound was deep and burned of hell fire, but she still had all her fingers. She knew she should have been terrified but she relaxed her shoulder in relief knowing that a clip across the arm was the extent of the damage.

Avery looked back in the direction of her attacker only to see a tail disappearing into the clouds. Rather than increasing his speed to chase, the Knight slowed its pace. His head swiveled slowly from side to side as he searched for any movement in the thick cloud cover that might give away his opponent. With hesitation to lift her hand once more, she sheathed Hemlock in order to hold a proper grip on the exposed bone.

"I don't think she'll be coming back soon," she yelled above the wind. "She's wounded. We all are."

Avery felt him huff and exhale beneath her legs in irritated agreement. That part was undoubtedly Moz and she couldn't help but smile. He dipped downward into the thick patch of clouds and the wet air felt cooling on her arm. They descended much slower than they had climbed the skies and minutes later the patchy treetops came back into view.

Moz circled the sky until they came upon the clearing they had left their friends in, though there were noticeably more bodies littering the ground than there had been when they departed. The flight had been smooth until just before impact, Avery's grip unhinged from the bone when they violently hit the ground and she soared over the Knight's neck.

Avery hit the ground skidding, her knife was yanked from her belt and her cloak tangled around her neck. Avery hissed in sharp pain as her wound screamed. She used her uninjured arm to prop herself up slowly to look back at the Knight. The blue titan had vanished and in its place was a bleeding Moz. His face was scraped and pink from hitting the ground, red dripping from his punctured black armor.

Her gaze shifted to the others. All of them were watching Moz in horror until Tristan's attention shifted to her and a silent panic washed over them both. Avery was the first to sense the danger and she pushed herself out of the mud, dashing to be the first one to reach Moz as she drew her sword. She heard feet pounding behind her as the rest of them ran towards Moz as well. The Knight was wounded and they wanted to finish the job.

"Y' DON'T UNDERSTAND! HE WOULD NEVER HURT ANY OF YA'!" Tristan shouted from behind her.

Avery had thought for sure Tristan would be the biggest advocate for slaughtering Moz with the way he spoke about demons - she found it was a relief to be wrong.

She quickly closed the distance between herself and where Moz was crumpled on the ground; his wounds looked even worse up close. Avery whirled around and wielded Hemlock in a defensive stance. Alice and Kurosaki had their biggest rifles drawn in their direction. As Avery stared down the long barrels, she prayed to the

Goddess for the first time in a long time; she hoped she was right.

When they stopped, Maria and Shank both had arrows ready as they flanked the sides of the group to shoot past Avery rather than through her. Tristan didn't halt when everyone else did and instead ran the five meters to stop beside her, turning to the others.

"Have y'lot lost your minds? This is Moz, for fuck's sake, he would never hurt any of ye'," he repeated, the desperation in his voice clear as day. No one lowered their weapons.

Alice was the first to speak. "He's been a Knight this whole time. Who's to say he isn't leading us to our deaths according to Morgana's design?"

"That's absurd and y'know it, Alice. Nobody wants to beat her more than Moz, NOBODY. Y' didn't see him that day."

"What are you blubbering about, you big baby?" Kurosaki's voice dripped with vitriol, a grimace smeared across his face.

"I was the one who found him… out in the field. I couldn't have been a month over eighteen. The boy was writhing in pain and screaming in sounds no man ever heard before. I went t'go exorcise him even though I barely knew what I was doin' and he screamed at me to get away, as far away as I could. I told him no and worked on him. When no demon left him, he said it wouldn't help… that he was a Knight of Od and that no one could save him. Y'know what I heard in his voice? Hopelessness. Not a trickster son of a bitch like y' would expect. This was someone that was trying to rip himself out of his own skin."

Kurosaki's eyes narrowed. "Then you knew he was a Knight this whole time."

"I did."

Kurosaki jabbed his gun at the air in Tristan's direction with hatred igniting in his ghostly face.

"You deceitful oaf… you put all of us in harm's way and I will make you both pay. I'll rip—"

"Listen to me, all of you!"

Avery stood with Hemlock kissing the palm of her hand in a threatening manner when they turned their attention to her. Maria was the first one to look horrified and she relaxed her hold on her arrow. Even though her blood had not been drawn, Avery felt the itch of the spirits below as they awaited to break the veil.

"Moz is the only shot we have to stand a chance against the rest of the Knights. We won't be able to retrieve the last one without him. I won't allow you to kill him… and do you really want to go through me?"

Even Kurosaki looked nervous at the threat and Avery began to understand how much leverage she had; how much the sword of Paion was feared. Shank hesitated before lowering their bow and the rest of the party followed their lead, though with obvious reluctance.

"Don't get the idea that you call the shots around here, cocky brat," Kurosaki said with snarled lips and it became easy for Avery to see which friend Moz shared his abrasiveness with. He turned around and began to storm back into town. Her gaze shifted to Maria, who was watching Moz with a quivering lip before meeting Avery's stare.

"Avery, you're right. If his goal really was to kill us… well, he had plenty of chances."

"Moz was the one who rounded us up anyway," Shank murmured, staring at the ground in front of Moz as they recalled memories. "What importance would we have for his goal to recruit us, to take us from our old lives if his goal was only to kill us? None of us were significant enough to be murdered so meticulously, so calculated. He wasn't going to kill us. Never."

"There are things worse than death," Alice cautioned before trailing her eerie companion. Maria ignored the comment and looked at Shank.

"Help me patch them up, he's in pretty bad shape."

Tristan was already lifting Moz off the ground to support his left side and Shank ducked under Moz's right arm to hold him up.

"Maria, go find the healer in town. We need to at least bandage him before we try to make him get back on Emory," they instructed, seeming to take calm authority to handle the situation.

She nodded upon Shank's instruction and sprinted on into the trees. Avery looked at Shank with a puzzled expression.

"I don't understand, why would we not let a healer help him completely?"

"I trust myself more than I trust the other healers in this town. I didn't count on a wound this severe happening and don't have enough in the saddlebag, we just need something to hold him together until we get home."

"What kind of healer doesn't travel with enough medical supplies," Avery's disapproval was much sharper than she had intended, though she knew Lily's contempt would be much worse if she were present.

Shank ignored the comment and instead said "Lead us into the town."

She nodded and drew Hemlock as her eyes met with Moz's for the first time since they crashed into the earth. Exhaustion clearly fogged his consciousness and the blood from his forehead pooled on top of his right eyebrow before dropping in beads.

"Kurosaki… and Alice," he spoke with a busted lip that dripped down his chin. "They're going to snipe us."

"We've already established that nothing they do can get y'to drop," Tristan declared. "Although that doesn't keep the three of us safe."

Avery had almost missed the ethereal face standing behind the men and her idea instantly clicked.

"Owen, round up any spirits hanging around this area. Go before us and see where the two snipers went.

Warn us if it looks bad," she then turned to Shank. "Can you ask Ina to do the same? Aegis will stick with us."

They nodded in confirmation and Ina disappeared into the wood. When their accompanying revenant had vanished as well, the group ventured back into the forest at a crawl. Moz's labored breathing was heard even over the pelting of rain droplets on leaves. Any light that had been able to peek out from the patches of clouds had become scarce.

Avery was thankful that Aegis was the first to speak. "*I suppose you do believe the possibility that Kurosaki and Alice would kill you all, is that correct?*"

She scanned the forest before each step. "I would like to give them the benefit of doubt, but I just can't."

Out of the corner of her eye she saw the cat duck under the fallen trunk she had merely stepped over. "*What are you going to do now that you know Moz is a Knight of Od?*"

"Sure we might have to be a little more cautious now, but nothing has changed. You knew this whole time, didn't you?"

"*Of course I did.*"

"And I suppose Ina did, didn't she?"

"More than likely, yes. Demons recognize one another instantaneously."

"They do?"

She heard only the throaty laugh. Avery paused and turned around to face the three men. "That's why Croxi attacked Moz," the conversation she had been having with Aegis was transferred over to them without any explanation. "Demons recognize one another and that's why. He was trying to protect Maria."

"Yes, that's quite an astute observation, Avery, but we have to keep going," Shank returned the agitation Avery had dished out earlier.

She turned and pressed on, but Aegis kept prying at her thoughts.

"Shall we place bets on the current state of Centralia? I bet the townsfolk had seen two beasts emerge from the sky and assumed a situation of apocalyptic proportion. Though they wouldn't be wrong."

CHAPTER EIGHT

THE CHARIOT

By the time they reached the heart of Centralia, Moz's feet were dragging against the ground as Shank and Tristan pulled him by his arms. He knew he wasn't dead, yet he felt he was barely able to call himself corporeal. Moz swore he was falling out of his skin and his dry throat would only croak when he tried to call out to his friends to push him back inside it. The throbbing in his head never ceased and the dark fog around the edges of his vision was a tide receding until it closed in on him once more.

Blurry Centralians were already tending to their dead and his ears winced at the sound of sobbing from every direction. A closer voice spoke, Shank? It sounded as though they mentioned a sniper. Moz flinched when the echo of the gunshot rang in his skull - he swore he would pay Kurosaki back.

"I thought for sure they were going to shoot at us, not Morgana's legion. I think we might owe them one," Avery's voice was the only one to break through with complete clarity, the soft tone was an inhale of relief until it was gone.

He didn't realize the thing living within him had stilled, watching her through his eyes. They widened with the realization of what had unfolded in that field, and he thrashed hard in the hands that gripped him. He squeezed his eyes shut as hard as he could to protect her from being watched by the thing within.

"You didn't expect that, did you Mozzy-boy?"

Their fingers gripped him harder to hold him more rigidly and the yelling was a dull buzz in his ear drums. It only wanted to listen to Avery. He didn't have to look up from the boots facing him to know she was looking at him with horror.

"She knows I'm here as much as you do, heeeee!"

Why had the demon latched itself onto her? He heard it call out to her even from behind that door when he had traded places with the Knight. She did not hear him banging his fists on the door and screaming to be let out. Moz didn't know which was worse: the fact that she listened or the fact that the Knight obeyed her every command. From where he was pushed back into his own skull, he watched the flight with his own eyes and heard the roars through his own ears but was somehow detached. The Knight had never taken full control before.

"That's right, Mozzy-boy. No more nosebleeds. It's all or nothing now."

He roared out in anger to the voice that only he could hear. The two friends that held him tightened their grips as though Moz was about to go berserk at any moment. He knew that it was a dangerous possibility, he had only confirmed it when he thrashed in anger again in retaliation to himself.

The fog around him went darker after he heard the creaking of a door swing open. Where were they taking him? A torture chamber, surely. He would stay there until they could devise a plan to kill him and the other Knights; he hoped they would succeed and he cried out for death. A crisp scent of burning white sage licked at his nostrils, stinging the demon within. Voices buzzed around him incoherently before he was lifted and placed stomach-down onto a bed.

His aching bones sunk into the feather mattress and his vision began to clear as he turned his head as far over his left shoulder as he could to see what was happening. An elderly woman was fussing over a shelf of bottles in his immediate line of sight. Though she was speaking, the ringing remaining in Moz's ears had not faded enough for him to understand what she was saying. The black dress she wore twirled as she turned to speak to someone else in the room. A low voice whispered in response to her bone-dry question. As he listened to the small world around him, a face leaned to the side as if to peek at Moz where he laid.

At the sight of Avery's face he felt the demon within his skull rumble one last time before it nodded off. His vision and hearing returned violently and he flinched at the sudden return of his senses. Moz turned himself onto his good shoulder, gasping for breath as he looked around him.

The room around him was as sloppily put together as the shack. Only a few candles illuminated the room darkened by its wood walls, had he somehow missed the day slipping into night? No windows were present to know for sure. The heavy rain that had pelted the ceramic shingled roof was beginning to taper off as the Knight sank into a slumber.

Shank was the first to meet Moz's stare, ducking to meet it first with a look of fear and then it shifted to concern. "Are you back?"

He still struggled to catch his breath but managed to nod his head. "She... she murdered the Priestess."

"An' we'll kill her for it. Don't y'worry about that, William."

The woman who was now approaching him with a dripping cloth said nothing, seeming to know better than to ask them any questions. She prompted Moz to turn back onto his stomach, and he sucked his teeth in pain as he wondered how he had propped himself up at all. The wound on his shoulder stung as a spirit of some kind stung at his skin and he yelled out before breathing harder.

As she turned around back to her shelf of medicinal herbs, he turned his head towards where

Avery sat in a chair at the opposite side of the small room.

"Why… did you do it," he choked out.

Her face froze at the question and her fingers around her knees visibly tightened as her mouth opened slightly before closing. He couldn't tell if her cheeks were flushed from the sudden demand or from the cold rain that still clung her wet hair to her face.

"I thought, I don't know what I thought. Something told me I was supposed to," she finally answered. "I know it doesn't make any sense, but it was like I didn't have any choice."

Moz swore abruptly and she flinched. He had been right in believing it wasn't just Avery making an obnoxiously dumb decision; the Knight pulled her. Anger heated his face and he wasn't certain if it was because of her or the beast that slept inside him.

"Avery," he knew his voice sounded far more stern than he had intended it to. "Because you have done that, he's never going to let go of you. If you ever resist his future pulls, I can't promise the Knight won't crush you. That's not me in there and I can't do anything to protect you. He will do it again because you listened the first time."

Her face paled and he felt a tinge of regret. If he had just kept the Knight out for a little longer, everything would have been alright.

"I didn't know," she murmured. Before he could answer, the woman who was tending to him spoke.

"I can't in good conscience let you leave in this condition. I recommend staying in that bed for the night and your friends can come fetch you in the morning."

"Do what y'need to," Tristan approved from the corner. Moz looked at his older friend and the deepening worry lines that he had not noticed before in his face. "We just need him in the morning."

Tristan began to shuffle out before he stopped and looked down at him. "Do y' want one of us to stay a while?"

"I can stay a while," Avery spoke and Moz tried to ignore the small prick of relief he felt. "I would just need someone to come back and show me the way."

"We'll send Maria down here once we find her. I'm sure she would like to know how he's doing. Be quiet company while he rests," Shank added the last sentence pointedly as though to verbally slap Moz's wrist for not having rested yet. Avery nodded dutifully and they turned to walk out the door, Tristan looking over his shoulder and waving before they both disappeared.

There was a heavy silence hanging on the room broken only by the occasional clink of glass vials that the stern woman tinkered with. His eyes closed as he controlled his breathing pattern to try to slow his heart rate to a comfortable pace. Wood creaked from the corner opposite him and Moz opened his left eye to peer into the dark room. Avery was shifting uncomfortably in her chair and ignoring an accusing stare from Aegis in her lap.

"Avery," he mumbled her name with all of the breath he could hold inside him at once to make sure he had her attention. "When you fought, it was remarkably terrifying. I was wrong… in every way. I was awful to you and I have no excuse. I would take it all back, but I can't. And for that… I will always be sorry."

When he expected her to bask in his admission with an "I told you so", he was met with a warm smile.

Hadn't he just managed to slow his heart rate down? *Oh, no.*

"I suppose now is as good of a time to start fresh as any. I forgive you," her response was soft. His shoulders sunk back into the mattress from where had held them rigid in the air. This couldn't be happening, not to him.

"Let me know if there's anything I can do to help," she added, shifting her gaze from Moz to the woman he had nearly forgotten about. She turned from her bottles to Avery and shook her head.

"Nothing needing help here."

Moz turned his head upwards so that he could speak without being muffled by the pillow. "Can you make sure Jack is okay?"

Avery nodded and stood up to approach the side of the cot. "Where is he?"

"I think Shank put him under the cot, but I can't hear him."

Avery knelt next to the cot and ducked to the floor to look underneath. He closed his eyes to avoid looking at her. Moz heard her fumble around beneath the wood frame of the cot, his breath catching in his throat as he became certain of what happened to his small companion.

"Yeah, he's fine," she finally whispered and he opened his eyes.

Avery held Jack in her open hand as she stroked the top of his head gently with her other pointer finger. Her lips were turned in a small smile, the dark lashes of her eyes stretching out to reach the faint freckles on her cheeks while she looked down at the rat. They turned upwards when she looked at him with steel blue eyes.

"Just sleepy is all," she added. "Do you want to hold him?"

"Sure, but-" he was cut off when Avery placed Jack into his left hand that was open and dangling to the floor from the short cot. The familiar heartbeat fluttered in his palm and Moz felt instantly comforted. Avery grinned; gods, she was getting on his nerves with the smiling.

Before he could resort to his reflex to snap at her, she stood up. "Try to sleep, too."

— ⟨← —

It didn't take long for Maria to track down where Kurosaki and Alice had hidden themselves, especially since they had chosen one of the buildings Sera had utilized in her escape from the temple grounds. Her fingers relaxed a little around the arrow she held in her bow as she stepped into the forgotten shop. She couldn't remember why the florist had abandoned the place until she noticed the crumbling lumber of the walls as she made her way through the empty racks. If she remembered correctly, there was a small apartment above the shop where the owner had lived. Was his name Tor? George? She couldn't remember.

Maria carefully ascended the creaking steps in a narrow hall at the back of the shop. When she rose high enough to see the floor of the top floor, she caught a glimpse of the end of a snake's tail before it vanished.

"Found you," she called out loudly enough for the pair to be able to hear her. The last thing she wanted was to successfully sneak up on Kurosaki and Alice; she didn't think she would make it out of that alive. She climbed into the empty loft to see Kurosaki kneeling on the floor in front of the window facing the street, the long barrel of his gun extending slightly from the threshold. Alice stood up and brushed off her black pants.

"You're slick, Cruz," she noted with a faint air of being impressed. "I wasn't expecting any of you to pin us down for at least another thirty minutes."

"Well, you did leave a hefty body count in your wake," Maria answered. "Good job, I guess."

Though the pair made her uneasy, she was glad they had eliminated as many of Morgana's legion as they did. She couldn't imagine what would have happened to Moz and the others if they hadn't. Maria just wished they were not the only ones with coveted guns from Eyon. She made a mental note to obtain firearms whenever they made it to the island, anything to level the playing field.

"Will you let him recover before you try to fight him?"

Maria saw no point in dancing around the obvious. They weren't going to sit still knowing that Moz was a Knight. Though it made her angry, she couldn't blame them. Simply acknowledging the fact he had been a Knight the whole time made her feel sick. She had thought she knew him inside and out. Alice gave her a smile with one hand on her bony hip as Mori began to slink around her leg in a coil.

"I suppose we could pardon him for a while, seeing as we shot the bastard and he just got back up."

"Thank you," she said in a soft voice before turning to leave. "We'll be waiting for you at home, I need to go find everyone."

She descended down the steps a little louder than she had climbed them and the wood cried out with each thump of her boots. Maria exited the depressed storefront into the town square that appeared to be in even worse shape.

Voices hushed around her and the eyes of strangers recognized her face. Centralians had begun to collect their dead, covering them in canvas sheets and lining them in a row in the middle of the square. She knew that this was where family members would rush to when they realized their loved ones had been gone for a suspicious while. Maria sucked in a breath of air to try to force out tension that had settled in the base of her spine, reminding herself that such a slaughter would have never happened at home.

Nobody ventured into the southern swamps of Wrencrest if they didn't have to. Her family was safe. She mentally slapped her wrist for thinking such selfish thoughts when a woman cried out at the foot of the canvas row, swaying with grief as she kneeled beside an uncovered body. Maria quickly walked in the opposite direction; she didn't need any reminder that this was their fault.

Maria's attention was quickly snatched by a darting shadow in her peripheral vision. She flinched to face it and caught a glimpse of the humanoid shadow before it disappeared. She swore out loud and broke into a run. Why did it take her so long to realize that souls were going to be hijacked?

The massacre made it incredibly easy for the fledgling demons to latch onto a stunned soul. Even though Centralia was not a crowded space and usually had nothing to offer them, they were going to appear out of every nook and cranny they had been hiding in for this sudden opportunity. There was no way she could slay them herself; the only person who had a blessed sword was wounded and nowhere to be found. And a Knight.

"I should… have healed… him myself," she heaved to herself. Her eyes rapidly scanned for the Leeches as she ran.

She almost made it to the other end of town before she heard a man call her name. Maria whipped around in fright and almost sank to the ground in relief when she saw Shank and Tristan chasing after her from an alley. She sprinted to them, throwing her arms around them both. Shank's bow was knocked out of their hand but they returned her embrace.

"This is all our fault," she cried out.

Tristan patted her head, his open hand easily covering the size of her entire crown. "We didn't kill those people, Maria. Morgana and Sera did. None of us knew they were already here."

"But I couldn't shoot down her familiar! It followed us because I couldn't kill it," she jumped out of their arms in anger, frustrated tears on her cheeks. Her face burned with anguish and part of her wanted to snap her bow in half, never to claim the status of an archer again.

"It wouldn't be fair of us to put sole responsibility on you. I missed, too," Shank put their hand on her shoulder. "Like you said, it was quite literally a shot in the dark."

She let out a sharp breath and squared her shoulders, knowing she needed to move on from the gnawing fact that she still had missed.

"Where's Moz and Avery?"

"With Jane," Tristan answered. "She reckons that he needs to be kept through the night. Avery volunteered to stay behind, but I reckon she would feel better if ya were there too."

Shank eyed her as though they were expecting her to explode, and she looked at them with narrowing eyes.

"I'm not going to do it, I need to get away from that."

They suddenly exploded with exasperation. "Come on, Maria! It's not going to kill you to just heal him! Avery's handling it just fine!"

Maria shook her head. She didn't know Avery before she took the gift from Balthazar and Mona but she still noticed the girl stepping further and further into the Land of the Dead in such a short amount of time. Even though her own gifts from Balthazar were for healing purposes, she had no intention of using them. Not after Firefly. She had stepped out of her bounds as a healing witch and into Avery's territory of dealing with the dead.

Simply the thought of Firefly's name made her swear she saw a parchment-pale figure watching her from the gap between Shank and Tristan's shoulders. She felt her own face drain of blood as she froze in terror. Shank lifted the back of their palm to her forehead and spoke, though she missed their words.

"Let Jane heal him without witchcraft," she blurted out. "If you're not satisfied, you do it. I won't use it."

Even though she knew simply healing Moz was a lot different than raising her friend from the dead, there was no way Maria was willing to take any risk. She set an arrow in her bow and took their silence as realizing her firm refusal.

"I spotted a Leech down by Maurice's. Be on the lookout and hold down the homestead," she said before running in the direction from where she came, towards Jane's Apothecary.

She reached the entry, her shoulders sagged with sudden relief before she knocked on the cracked door. Maria stared at the peeling mint paint before the door was cracked open and Jane's face peeked out. When the woman saw Maria her old face folded even more with a smile.

"I haven't seen you in a while, lovie. Why don't you come on inside," she invited before she kissed Maria on the cheek with a warm greeting. Before Jane let her pass the threshold she put her spidery fingers up against her face to whisper "Your friends haven't been much company, to be frank."

Maria cracked a small smile before stepping inside. The apothecary was more of a small room than a shop, held in the bottom floor of Jane's home. Jane immediately went back to her work station after letting Maria in. The woman stood at a repurposed bureau that stood up to Jane's sternum, the top covered in assorted glass jars of every color imaginable. The farthest corner of the room was illuminated by the few pillar candles on a small table in the middle of the room and Maria saw the sagging body in the cot.

Even in sleep Moz looked utterly defeated. His arm was hanging off the side of the cot and the back of his hand lay against the gnarled rug on the floor; Jack slept curled in his open palm. The black cloak had been removed from around his neck to reveal the wound underneath the punctured armor. Jane had already cleaned the congealed blood to provide access to the torn flesh. Maria stepped closer to take a look.

"He's very lucky it wasn't any deeper," Jane said from behind her before shooing Maria away from the bedside. "Sit with your other friend."

Maria had almost forgotten Avery was there. She spun around to see her sitting in the corner opposite Moz's, sideways in the wooden chair with her legs draped over the left arm. Aegis was curled up on her stomach and asleep, she guessed, from the lack of eerie eyes looking back at Maria. His Reaper did not give her the same courtesy.

"He fell asleep not too long ago," Avery said in a soft voice. "Jack, too."

Maria had almost settled in comfortably on the floor with her back against the wall when Avery prodded her in the shoulder once and whispered her name.

"What?"

When Maria turned to look at her, Avery gestured around her own head with a hand swooping from her left shoulder to her right one before pointing towards Jane's back. Maria exaggerated her confused look to match Avery's vague pantomiming. The other Reaper's shoulders dropped and she huffed in slight frustration; whatever she was trying to communicate was apparently not meant to be overheard. Avery tapped her chin twice in thought before her face lit up in a sudden stroke of genius.

Avery pointed to Hemlock's sheath propped against the corner that the back of her chair straddled, grabbing it and shaking it once before setting it back down. She slashed her arm through the air with a flat palm, the displaced air whooshing close to Maria's face as she watched in confusion. Avery pointed her finger with a jab in Jane's direction, then once more made the gesture around her head.

Maria's bottom jaw sunk fast. Avery was trying to illustrate a Reaping. The sword, the designating aura around those to be collected. Jane was going to die soon and Avery was to be the one to collect her.

Her heart fluttered in panic, when was she to die? Within the week or as she tried to heal Moz? Maria winced again at her selfishness with her eyes blinking hard in attempt to push it away.

Avery's expression was gloomy and she was wringing her hands in her lap, the stirring aroused Aegis from his sleep. Did Avery feel guilty for the assignment? How long had she even been a Reaper? Maria eyed her curiously before standing up.

"Jane, will you allow me to help? You seem to be working quite hard," she forced her voice to sound eager rather than shocked or upset.

"That would be wonderful, lovie!"

Before Maria stepped up to the jars and supplies, she turned and looked down at Avery in a commanding stare. Avery understood immediately: no Reaper will touch Jane until Moz was healed.

Lily's boots hit the pebbly beach with a series of crunches. The crew ahead of her only half-wielded their weapons and was unsure what lay beyond the stony bank that rose from the shore. Morgana was the last to exit the last rowboat and she glanced back over her shoulder at the vessel they had left farther out in the sea before she sharply exhaled through her nostrils in impatience.

"Dusk is falling soon and still my bird has not returned," the captain said and turned to meet Lily's stare. Morgana pushed past her to begin following her crew up the bank. Lily thought of the peregrine falcon Morgana had handled days ago on the ship – what significance could it possibly have? Shortly before they came ashore Morgana had cast it into the air with evident purpose.

Lily followed the path in the rocks that the crew members before her had taken, lodging her right foot on a small ledge and using her arms to pull herself up. When she reached the top she was surprised by the dark grass beneath her feet.

"We have no time to waste!" Peter had scaled the bank behind her and ran past Lily to follow the rest of the crew.

Lily unhooked the bow from her shoulder where she had hung it to climb with both hands. She followed the officers closely, an arrow resting between her fingertips if danger arose.

The crew traveled with a hasty pace into the early hours of the night. When the dark of the night became too thick to see through they lit metal lanterns on long handles. Lily's hearing began to compensate for the lack of perfect sight and the small sounds the forest held sent her flinching at the smallest snap or crack.

A flash of green reflected the glow of the lanterns from somewhere in the thick of trees ahead of them. Out from the brush emerged a gray timber wolf, easily larger than any dog Lily had ever seen. She stopped in her tracks to stay as still as she possibly could. The large animal was bounding toward them, yet nobody ran.

"Look out!" Lily shrieked, perhaps they had not spotted the wolf as easily as she had.

When no one reacted, she raised her bow to aim at the beast. If she couldn't outrun it, perhaps she could hit it in a vital area and give everyone time to run. Peter shoved her bow to the side before she had even seen him approach her and Lily looked at him with angry bewilderment.

"The wolf is with us, it belongs to our eyes from inland," he said.

"What the fuck do you mean the wolf is with us? It's a bloody animal and you-" she cut herself off abruptly when she saw the animal break its run and slowly approach Morgana.

Though her feet seemed to be made of concrete blocks, Lily inched towards them to figure out why the animal had simply stopped. No gnashing teeth, no ripping skin, not even a growl to prompt the woman to step away. Morgana was crouched down low on her feet before it and Lily flinched hard when she saw the woman lift a hand to the furry neck gently.

"Wh... what is going on here?"

"We offered you the safety of your friend, not an interview," Lily was thankful that Morgana didn't turn to see her uneasy stare.

Before Lily could retort with a furious comment, Morgana stood up and began running in the direction the wolf had come from. As she ran, the canine followed close at her heels.

"She's up here! Crew, hurry!"

The wolf led the hurried group of officers, with Morgana keeping a close pace behind the animal. Lily struggled to keep up with Iggy and Peter as they ran through the trees. Branches cracked in every direction under the dozens of feet with only the sound of Lily's heartbeat pounding behind her ears competing for the loudest noise.

Who was up ahead? It seemed Morgana's icy demeanor was shattered by fear as the captain searched frantically through the trees.

Quick seconds passed by when the cries of frustration fell upon the ears of the crew. From around Iggy's large frame she saw a glimmer of red movement. Lily didn't see what was happening when she heard Morgana cry out with a startling show of relief.

"Sera!"

The officers in front of her slowed to a halt, Lily and everyone else behind her coming forward to see what was happening. She peeked around Iggy to see Morgana trying to help a young woman stand.

The injured woman had striking red hair, as vibrant as Morgana's, tumbling down her shoulders in waves. It was even more striking against her dark clothing, black leather armor plates with grommets of gold and black pants. A cloak of inky green covered her back and spilled lopsided over her left shoulder, clearly the result of a tussle. She was clutching her right side with her left hand and hissing in pain when Morgana coaxed her into lifting it so she could take a look at the damage. Crimson glimmered beneath her shirt and stained the palm and slender fingers that she held skyward.

"Sera, who did this to you?" The rage in Morgana's voice was terrible and thick.

"They call her the Berserker Witch, Mother," Sera hissed. "One of Mona and Balthazar's bitches, only this one can bend the dead as she pleases."

Lily looked amongst the officers around her to see if any of them appeared as confused as she was. Not confusion, but anger rested on their hard faces. With the rage she heard coating Morgana's words she did not dare to ask for clarification.

"Why, that meddling bastard," Morgana snarled her lips in disgust at the strange name. "Do we know who she is?"

"There was Mosley, his exorcist, Kurosaki, and Shank. There were three women I had not encountered before and know not of their names, the witch was one of them."

Sera, the injured woman, looked up at Morgana with a sudden shift from anger to alarm. "Mother, she was working with the Knight. As allies."

Morgana suddenly straightened with wide eyes. "The Knight? You mean he broke free?"

Sera nodded. Her mother turned around and looked at the crew behind her with the most sinister smile Lily had seen yet.

"We get this young woman to Miss Porter as soon as possible so we may pursue another objective. Ladies and gentlemen, we're bagging us a witch."

HEMLOCK EXCERPT

Mud mixed with the blood oozing out of Avery's busted bottom lip as she was dragged across the unforgiving terrain of the earth. Her cries for help were drowned out by the shouting men as they pulled the other end of the rope wrapped tightly around both of her wrists. The villagers of Centralia emerged from their homes to see the Berserker Witch being punished; their expressions turning into sick smiles of joy.

Only hours before they had been ravaged by the Beldam's Legion - the murder of the High Priestess led by Sera. Avery hadn't been quick enough to keep the body count low and she was being dragged off to die. No, that wasn't it; she attracted the deaths like moths to a flame. It wasn't enough to carry souls off to the afterlife as a Reaper, Balthazar made her into a witch so she could bend them to her will. "Necromancer" was the word Moz had used.

"AEGIS!" She shrieked again, hoping the cat would hear her.

He might not have been able to free her on his own, but he could have warned Moz or the other demon companions. But her familiar was nowhere to be found.

Avery's legs kicked and flailed, desperately trying to anchor herself in place by burying the heels of her boots in the slick mud. She failed to ground herself as her feet were uprooted and carried with the rest of her.

"OWEN!"

Even the solemn revenant that Balthazar had left in her care was absent. Fucking useless. She turned her sore neck towards the man carrying her sword on his back. Hemlock. If there was any way she could get it and slice her palm, feed it a blood sacrifice- these fuckers will pay.

"String her up there!"

Avery's eyes widened and she struggled to look behind her. She was suddenly dropped to the ground and the friction re-opened the cuts on her scraped cheek. At first she thought they were heading into an open mouth of darkness until the light from a crackling torch revealed the first trunks of the forest.

"Fuckin' ironic," she said out loud with blood dribbling down her chin.

She had survived the perils of the forest only to be dragged back into it with a death sentence. Demons, Reapers, even death by starvation would have been bearable. If she died by the hands of these men, Avery hoped no one would find her body; it would be far too embarrassing.

The mob stopped at the foot of a large oak and a man closed a grubby fist around the collar of Avery's cloak to pull her up to her feet. She choked on the sudden pressure around her windpipe and he grinned at her with half-rotted teeth before shoving her towards the tree. A much leaner man, perhaps not even much older than she was, took the end of the ropes and tossed it over a low-hanging limb of the tree. Other hands joined him, using all of their weight to pull backwards and lift Avery off her feet. Her wrists crunched with pain and she wailed in agony.

"Douse 'er!"

Maurice, the drunkard Moz had lifted money from the night before, stepped forward and began flinging a dark bottle to splash Avery with its contents. A sickly-sweet scent of alcohol curled around her nostrils and her eyes bugged out of her skull with panic.

"LET ME GO!"

She thrashed as hard as she could, hoping that the ropes would break under the strain of her weight. Instead of a captive about to break free, she felt more like a flopping fish pulled out of the sea and dangled like a prize.

As the largest of the men held the other end of the ropes, the others closed in around her, drawing nearer and nearer with their torches. Her blood was boiling from the heat and she squeezed her eyes shut as she waited for her fiery end.

The air split with a loud crack that echoed off the trees, followed by a heavy squish on the muddy earth. Avery fell hard to the ground when the rope was suddenly slackened and she slipped face first in the slick muck. She lifted her head and saw the man keeping the rope was now on the ground, the side of his head completely gone as he lay in a puddle of gory matter and blood.

ACKNOWLEDGEMENTS

This book wouldn't have been possible without a few friends - quite literally.

Cappy: thank you for pointing out that I'm a comma fiend. I am sad to report that while there is no cure, you were the genius who reigned me in. You taught me so much about being a better storyteller and while there is still much to learn, I will value that forever.

Mary: my #1 cheerleader, you were the friend who kept me going. Thank you for answering all my bizarre questions with enthusiasm and always breathing down my neck for the next book.

My other test readers, Julie and Stoney: thanks for sticking with the book from its early dumpster-fire stages through the final cuts. Thank you to my family for being unsurprised by the strangeness and rooting for me through it all.

And thanks to Rob Zombie, Johnny Hollow, and Marika Hackman for the bitchin' music to write to.

ABOUT THE AUTHOR

Elle Samhain is from the Seattle area and began writing *The Shintori Chronicles* while earning their Bachelor of Fine Arts at Washington State University. They are active in the pagan and queer communities, which have impacted both their writing and visual arts.

If they're not writing or making resin collages, they're probably binge watching *The X-Files* or talking to cats in sing-song.

www.ingramcontent.com/pod-product-compliance
Lightning Source LLC
Chambersburg PA
CBHW011149310726
48973CB00010B/2833